I0824434

A LYLE SAXON READER

A LYLE SAXON READER

LOST STORIES OF THE FRENCH QUARTER AND BURIED TREASURE

LYLE SAXON

Edited by
JAMES MICHAEL WARNER

Publisher's Cataloging-in-Publication data

Names: Saxon, Lyle, 1891-1946, author. | Warner, James Michael, editor.

Title: A Lyle Saxon reader : lost stories of the French Quarter and buried treasure / Lyle Saxon ; edited by James Michael Warner.

Description: Includes bibliographical references. | First Hardcover Edition | St. Louis, MO: Cultured Oak Press, 2018.

Identifiers: ISBN 978-0-6921415-2-6 | LCCN 2018951163

Subjects: LCSH Short stories, American--Louisiana--New Orleans. | Vieux Carré (New Orleans La.)--Fiction. | New Orleans (La.)--Fiction. | Buried treasure--Fiction. | Louisiana--Description and travel--Fiction. | Louisiana--Social life and customs--Fiction. | BISAC FICTION / Short Stories (single author) | FICTION / Historical / General | FICTION / Southern

Classification LCC PS3537.A9756 L95 2018 | DDC 813/.52--dc23

Cultured Oak Press, 8816 Manchester Rd. #133, St. Louis, MO 63144 USA

www.culturedoak.com

info@culturedoak.com

To Connie

CONTENTS

INTRODUCTION

New Orleans author Lyle Saxon frequently told friends that he was a native of Baton Rouge, Louisiana, and though he seldom spoke of his childhood, he occasionally implied that he had spent the summers of his youth on an idyllic family plantation, and winters attending school in the city. These were mostly falsehoods, but they established the story that he wanted to live.

The facts, or what can be learned of them, are more interesting than the fibs. He was born in New Whatcom, Washington to Katherine "Kitty" Chambers and Hugh Allen Saxon. You can understand the fiction that Saxon told about his origins when you consider two things: Hugh completely abdicated participation in the life of his son, and from his earliest days, Saxon was in love with the state of Louisiana. By creating his childhood fantasy, Saxon constructed a novelist's life.

Hugh was a young correspondent on a New Orleans newspaper at the time he met Kitty, and she was a clerk in her father's Baton Rouge, Louisiana book shop.[1] They married in December 1890, only a short time after they met, and immediately took off to travel California and the Pacific Northwest. Hugh's mother, Elizabeth Lyle Saxon, lived in New Whatcom, Washington, and it was there, on April 4, 1891, that

Kitty gave birth to a boy whom she named Lyle Saxon.[2] But Hugh had already left his wife, for reasons that are not clear, and he may not even have been present for the delivery.

BIRTH RETURN.

1. Name of Child (a) Lyle Saxon
2. Date of Birth Sep 4th 1891
3. Place of Birth New Whatcom
4. Sex Male
5. Color (b) white
6. Alive ~~or Still-born~~
7. Legitimate ~~or Illegitimate~~
8. Mother's Maiden Name Kittie Chambers
9. Mother's Age Last Birthday 23
10. Color (b) White
11. No. of Child Born to this Mother 1st
12. Mother's Birthplace (c) La.
13. Father's Name Hugh A. Saxon
14. Father's Age Last Birthday 23
15. Color (b) White
16. Father's Occupation Correspondent
17. Father's Birthplace La

State of Washington, County of Whatcom, ss.

I hereby certify that the above is a true return of the said Birth, and of the other facts there recorded.

Dated at New Whatcom, Washington, this 24 day of Sep 1891

J. M. Lawrence M. D. (d)

NOTE.—(a) Give surname and Christian name, if child has been named.
(b) State color distinctly, so race may be known, as White, Black, Mulatto, Indian, Chinese, Mixed White and Indian, etc.
(c) Give State or foreign country, so nationality is plainly shown.
(d) If returned by any other than Physician, sign as: Accoucheur, Parent, Coroner, etc.

(OVER.)

Some years later Hugh re-married, so it is likely that he and Kitty divorced not long after Saxon's birth. It is not surprising that, for the rest of his life, Saxon held a grudge against his father because of the abandonment, and even years later he refused meetings when Hugh tried to visit him in New Orleans.[3]

The situation was fine meat for the gossips in Baton Rouge. They saw Kitty travel with a handsome man to the West Coast for several months and return with a newborn and no husband, so many concluded that the child was born out of wedlock. Furthermore, there is no evidence that Hugh visited his family in Baton Rouge, and he chose instead to reside in California where he worked for the *Los Angeles Herald* newspaper. But whispers along the Baton Rouge grapevine about Saxon's birth were simply wrong. First, his parents' marriage on December 10, 1890 is recorded in the Orleans Parish Marriage License Index. Second, the official report of Saxon's birth in Whatcom County, Washington (the "Birth Return") clearly marked the delivery as "Legitimate," meaning that Kitty and Hugh were married at the time of the birth.[4]

When Kitty and her son returned to Baton Rouge, they moved in with her father, Mike Chambers, at 329 St. Louis Street. Under the pressures of a broken home and the bleating of the gossips, Saxon made up details about his imagined Baton Rouge birth and summers on a family plantation by the Mississippi River. In reality, Saxon apparently had a pleasant-enough childhood, though he spoke little of it later in life. His two maternal aunts, Lizzie and Maude, lived in the same household and helped to raise him, and his paternal grandparents, Elizabeth and Lyddell Saxon, stayed in contact. Elizabeth had a fascinating background, and became a significant influence in the boy's life. She was a celebrated feminist and suffragist in the late nineteenth and early twentieth centuries, and had been a writer for the *New Orleans Times* in the 1870s and 1880s.[5] In 1892, she helped to found the Portia Club, which was the first organization in New Orleans for the support of women's suffrage. And she lobbied and spoke across the nation in support women's rights. But her civic calling was not limited to politics; during a yellow fever outbreak, she organized a group called the Physiological Society, and through it recruited women to perform field work to stop the epidemic.[6]

Saxon was a precocious and intelligent boy. At the age of sixteen, he enrolled at Louisiana State University in Baton Rouge where he studied for five years, but reportedly quit just three hours shy of a baccalaureate.[7] Thereafter, he traveled about the South and Midwest for several years, mostly working as a journalist. But eventually he landed in New Orleans to work as a reporter, first at the *New Orleans Item*, and then settling in with the *Times-Picayune*. One of his earliest by-lines in the latter paper was above a long-remembered front-page article about the burning of the French Opera House in December 1919.

In the early 1920s, Saxon wrote some short stories and character sketches for the *Times Picayune*, including two serialized sagas. One of the serials, a forty-nine-part epic entitled, *At the Gates of Empire*, was about the descendants of a fictional French family named Beaumont and their lives among the most notable figures in New Orleans history.[8] Although serialized, it was probably Saxon's first novel-length published writing.

Saxon stayed at the *Times-Picayune* until 1926, and during that time he became the paper's most-read and respected theatrical and literary critic. Here Saxon developed close relationships with many ground-breaking writers of the age, including William Faulkner, William Spratling, Sherwood Anderson, Carl Carmer, Grace King, Roark Bradford and others who lived in or passed through New Orleans. Spratling and Faulkner even included Saxon in their tongue-in-cheek book, *Sherwood Anderson and Other Famous Creoles*, in which a cartooned Saxon relaxed upon an embroidered cushion to examine a paper entitled, "Eminent Victorians." The drawing's caption described, "Lyle Saxon: The mauve decade in Saint Peter Street."[9]

During the late 1910s and early 1920s, Saxon developed a deep love for New Orleans, and especially the French Quarter. Here he began a life-long effort to preserve the architectural integrity of the Quarter. A catalyst that spurred this effort was the tragic burning of the French Opera House in the cockcrow hours of December 4, 1919. Saxon lived only blocks from this structure, and sitting tearfully on the curb that early morning with close friends, he watched the old building come down.[10]

Directly as a result of this architectural and cultural loss, Saxon began an earnest advocacy for the preservation of the French Quarter. As a genial person, he made friends and supporters easily and used his journalism platform to build alliances with preservationists throughout the city. For example, on June 6, 1920, Saxon published an article entitled, *Vieux Carré Awakening; Is Coming Into Own Again*, in which he argued that house-hunters were once again scanning the real estate ads for "hidden beauties of architecture" in the Quarter.[11] In that article, without citing supporting evidence, he reported that young home buyers were flocking back to the French Quarter, seeking low housing prices, modern conveniences and beautiful streets. He also spoke warmly of his dear friend and French Quarter artist, Alberta Kinsey and of the flourishing art group that she nurtured—a band that later gelled to become the New Orleans Arts and Crafts Club. He even mentioned that Mrs. George Westfeldt, socialite, preservationist, and owner of the popular Green Shutter Tea Room, had recently purchased a historic mansion on Bourbon Street. This and other articles were publicity pieces designed to make the French Quarter appear to be the fashionable place to live. Saxon had begun a campaign that he would pursue for the rest of his life.

Saxon contributed to literary New Orleans for several years while working on the *Times Picayune*, and eventually convinced his editors to start an arts criticism column entitled, "Literature and Less." This series was well-received by the paper's readership, and helped to solidify Saxon's reputation as a cultivated personality. But eventually he tired of the restrictions on format and subject matter that newspapers required. In 1926 Saxon quit the *Times-Picayune* and moved to Greenwich Village in New York, believing that relocating to the major publishing center of the country was necessary to foster his writing career. After several lean months, he received a commission from the Century Company publishing house, under which he traveled back to Louisiana to report firsthand on the devastating flood of the Mississippi River in 1927. From this experience, he produced his first book, *Father Mississippi* (1927). Over the next years, he wrote three more books in quick succession, each about New Orleans and Louisiana: *Fabulous New Orleans* (1928), *Old Louisiana* (1929) and *Lafitte the Pirate* (1930). In these volumes he was not afraid to take a storyteller's liberty with facts and dialogue, but the books met with critical success and sold well. This was a busy period, for in addition to the books, he published several stories in New York-based magazines. Between 1927 and 1932, Saxon traveled frequently from New York to Louisiana, where he often spent time at Melrose Plantation. Eventually, homesickness got the best of him and in 1932, he left New York permanently to return to New Orleans and Melrose.[12]

The Works Progress Administration's Federal Writers Project hired Saxon in 1935 to oversee the production of *The New Orleans City Guide* (Houghton Mifflin, 1938), the purpose of which "is to present as complete a picture as possible of New Orleans within the limits of a volume that is not too unwieldy."[13] Saxon's skills in directing that volume convinced the Project to commission him for another guidebook, *Louisiana: A Guide to the State* (Hastings House), that published in 1941. This was followed by *Gumbo Ya-Ya* (Houghton Mifflin, 1945), co-edited by Saxon, Robert Tallant and Edward Dreyer.

By all accounts, Saxon played well his role as a genteel Southern author. Although in most cases his stories presented highly dramatized historical events—and sometimes fiction masquerading as history—Saxon developed a popular reputation as unofficial historian laureate for New Orleans. He played this role well also, and used it to further enhance the city's national reputation as a tourist destination, and to protect the city's architectural heritage. He was a man who loved and was loved by a city.

While preparing the Federal Writers Project guides, Saxon turned his thoughts to a long-time goal: the completion of a full novel about life in rural Louisiana. The result was *Children of Strangers* (Houghton Mifflin), which he published in 1937. Not counting the serial *At the Gates of Empire*, this was Saxon's first novel, and it was a significant departure from his other books. Although many of Saxon's writings represented people of color as cartoonish or two-dimensional background figures, *Children of Strangers* contained well-developed characters across a racial spectrum and made an often-painful examination of the effects of color barriers in rural Louisiana. The book met with wide critical success, although some Southern newspapers took a parochial view.[14] Despite the paternalistic—and sometimes degrading—approach with which many of his other writings portrayed African Americans and Native Americans, some viewed him as progressive for the age. For example, in 1936 Saxon succeeded in appointing a number of African American writers to positions at the Federal Writers Project, despite an ongoing budget crisis.[15]

Saxon continued to write about and celebrate his beloved city for several more years, but failing health sapped his energy. He passed away on April 9, 1946 after a long battle with cancer, only five days after his 54th birthday, and barely a month after he narrated the Rex Parade on nationwide radio for that year's Mardi Gras celebration. At the time of his death, he had been working on an autobiography. The book was published posthumously in 1947 under the title, *The Friends of Joe Gilmore and Some Friends of Lyle Saxon*, with additional stories by Saxon's friend, Edward Dreyer.

All stories in the present volume are selected from Saxon's early writing career between December 1919 and June 1923, and each was originally published in the *Times-Picayune* nearly a century ago. They represent interesting examples of his early writing style, and provide a contrast to his more mature works such as *Children of Strangers*. Except as noted below, these stories have not been in print since their original publication. I have grouped them into three categories: Short Stories, essays on Architectural and Cultural Preservation, and Character Sketches.

For further information about the life of Lyle Saxon, the reader should purchase two well-written books: *The Life and Selected Letters of Lyle Saxon*, by Chance Harvey (Pelican Publishing Company, 2003), and *Lyle Saxon: A Critical Biography*, by James W. Thomas (Summa Publications, 1991).

Short Stories

The first story in this section, *Who Would Go Hunt for Spanish Doubloons and Pieces of Eight?* is an unusual story for Saxon. The narrator, apparently Saxon himself, tells of finding a man hidden on a barrier island off the coast of Pensacola, Florida. The man has a fatal illness, but before he dies, he imparts to the narrator a treasure map, a cryptic diary and a promise of fabulous buried Spanish gold. All Saxon has to do is figure out what the clues mean. The whole episode is thoroughly tongue-in-cheek, and allows insight into Saxon's personality as a jokester. Although the first few paragraphs derive from the author's experience as a substitute teacher in Pensacola, the story published without any warning that it is fictional.[16]

Each of the next two short stories is only a few hundred words long. The first is *An Interlude*, and it presents a seemingly weak-willed husband who dithers between emotions for his wife. The second story is *The Forgotten Cigarette*, a work of flash fiction that casts a dim light on a neglectful parent. Although the events in these stories are not autobiographical, the reader may interpret each as a projection of Saxon's anger over his father's abandonment.

Many of the other stories in this section are poeticized accounts of interviews or current events, and Saxon did not shy from adding fictional plot twists and dialog. The story in *Reprieved* follows upon real-life news reports that a man named Angelo Guirlando was found guilty of murdering his brother-in-law, Henry Amato. According to an account of the crime reported in the *Times-Picayune*:

> Guirlando went to Independence [Louisiana] from Rockford, Ill., in July, 1921, and married Jennie Nicolosi, sister of Henry Amato's wife. He carried her with him to Rockford, but returned alone in December.

> He remained in Independence several days without seeing his sister or brother-in-law. December 10, however, these came into town from their home several miles away. Guirlando returned to their home and slept that night.
>
> The next morning the two men returned to Independence, according to the supreme court decision declaring Guirlando guilty, ate breakfast together and were smoking on the sidewalk when Guirlando opened fire upon Amato.
>
> Amato had requested a match from a passerby and was talking when Guirlando emptied the entire magazine of a pistol into his body. He then rushed to the dying man with a drawn knife shouting "deshonorato." He charged that Amato had criminally assaulted his (Guirlando's) wife, six days before the two were married.[17]

During and after the trial, Guirlando developed behaviors that caused psychiatrists, "alienists," they were called, to question his sanity. Such behaviors included constant fidgeting and utter non-responsiveness to questions or physical contact. Most jurisdictions had long-standing case law that prevented execution of insane inmates, even if that insanity arose after the crime. Under this doctrine, however, if an inmate returned to mental competency, the execution could be carried out. After Saxon's story published, the court judged Guirlando insane and sent him to the State Asylum for Criminal Insane in Jackson, Louisiana. But in a statement reiterating state law, Governor John Parker pronounced that if Guirlando ever recovered from his mental illness, the state would execute him. The result of this doctrine has been summarized this way: "Congratulations! You are cured. Now we will kill you."[18]

Saxon's next story, *Fingers in the Dark* resembles pulp fiction. It is based in part upon the account of real-life morphine addict Grace Gardiner who, in March 1923, arranged to have herself arrested on loitering charges so that she might go through withdrawal in the relatively safe environment of Orleans Parish Prison.[19] According to reports, she wanted to be freed of her seventeen-year-long addiction so that she could reunite with her four-year-old son. The

Times-Picayune followed her case with daily interviews and articles for a week, and then published four monthly updates. *Fingers in the Dark* is a first-person short story in which Saxon allegedly pays a street addict to buy morphine so that he can witness her shoot up in a filthy back-alley parlor. The addict tells Saxon that street vendors whose businesses were damaged by Gardiner's new-found fame would make a point of getting her re-hooked once she left prison. The story apparently sparked a concern with police that drug dealers would target Gardiner to get her back on morphine the moment she was back on the street, so they kept her in protective custody for a couple of months longer than they had initially planned.[20] She was finally released in late June, 1923, but not before she was allowed to make in-person appearances at a local department store.[21] It is not clear whether Saxon actually participated in the back-alley transaction, or whether it was a largely fictional story.

Saxon was not above recycling material or imagery that he thought worked well in previous stories. In the opening paragraphs of *Reprieved*, the author focuses on the senses of smell, sight and touch to create a feeling of closeness, and of being trapped:

> The prison odor is in the air; the smell of men, caged.
>
> Upon the edge of his bed a man is sitting, twisting his fingers in and out. Dirty fingers, with uncut, blackened nails. In and out.[22]

He uses practically the same scene in *Fingers in the Dark*—published only seven days after *Reprieved* appeared—in order to achieve that same feeling of being trapped in a tight space:

> The smell of food is in the air, mixed with that other prison odor, the odor of men, caged.... Her eyes are green, like sea-washed jade, her hair is vivid gold; but there are lines around her eyes, deep lines at the corners of her tight-lipped mouth. As she talks, she clasps and unclasps her fingers on her lap.[23]

In each case, the inmate is trapped not so much by the prison walls, but rather by the limitations of his or her troubled mind.

The Last Reunion is a poignant story of the few remaining soldiers who had fought in the Civil War. Each Spring, the surviving Confederate soldiers held a reunion in a Southern city, and in April 1923, it was New Orleans' turn. The veterans are shown as infirm and nearly-forgotten seniors, who pass away one by one from a world in which their relevance is no longer clear.

The main figure in *Well! He's Married Now* was a real-life New Orleans barefooted character who called himself the "Prophet Otto Marti," and he claimed to be a biblical seer. A year after Saxon wrote this story, the Prophet found himself on the losing end of a landlord's eviction lawsuit. After refusing to leave the house, he took a bullet in his still-bare foot during an altercation with the police. Two years later, he was in jail again for assaulting a roommate who had interjected herself in a violent argument between Marti and his wife.[24]

The final short story, *The One Thing*, casts an ironic light on truthfulness between two people in love.

New Orleans History and Preservation

After the fire that brought down the French Opera House, Saxon wrote a long line of stories that supported cultural and architectural preservation efforts of New Orleans. Saxon was a leader, and arguably the creator, of the city's architectural preservation movement of the 1920s and 1930s. It is certain that many historic structures in the Quarter stand today only because of his efforts, and because he projected a national spotlight on the neighborhood.

The first few paragraphs of *French Opera House to Rise Again from Ruins* were re-published in Chapter XXIX of Saxon's 1928 book, *Fabulous New Orleans*. To retain its context, the present volume reproduces the article in its entirety. As we approach 2019, the centennial of the French Opera's destruction, Saxon's full report helps to refresh our knowledge of what the monument represented to contemporary residents of New Orleans. Saxon embellished the opening and closing paragraphs of the article with florid descriptions of the fire and its aftermath, yet the story was well-received by saddened readers. The mid-text of the article, however, is factual and detailed, showing a sharp contrast in his writing styles. Despite Saxon's earnest promises in the article, politics and finances prevented the rebuilding of the French Opera.

An extensively re-worked version of the next story, *Charm of Old French Quarter Quickly Settles Upon Its Visitors*, appeared as Chapter XXVIII ("An Afternoon Walk") in *Fabulous New Orleans*. In each of these versions, the storyteller offers a guided tour, through the misty eyes of Saxon himself, from Canal Street down Royal Street to the Court House, and then to Jackson Square, where the guide takes his leave. The opening paragraphs of the two versions are almost identical, except that the original newspaper story is addressed to an imagined tourist who visits New Orleans for the first time. There, Saxon repeatedly refers to the reader as his "friend tourist." But the story in *Fabulous New Orleans* drops this practice entirely, perhaps because Saxon's editor found it pretentious. And *Fabulous New Orleans* contains expanded details. For example, Saxon repeats the old theory that the word "Dixie" originated from the antebellum New Orleans French term "dix," which was Creole jargon for a ten-dollar note.[25] Mercifully absent from the re-worked version, however, are the overused ellipses and serial asterisks that litter Saxon's early writings. He used these devices to add emphasis to a passage, but they were actually off-putting and have been edited out of the current volume. Comparison of the two story versions provides insights into how much his writing style matured over just a few years.

Character Sketches

In 1922 Saxon produced two regular but short-lived columns that focused solely on sketching the characters of New Orleans personalities. The first column had the uninspiring title, *Choosing a Vocation*, and it ran almost daily from March 27 through April 22, 1922. The articles offered short interviews with New Orleanians, most of whom were well-known, or were at least prominent within their social or business milieu. For the most part these stories were dry and to-the-point, but a few that were interesting are included in this volume.

In the series entitled, *Unusual Ways of Making a Living*, there were no stories in the sense of having a plot and a conclusion; these were pure sketches of true and odd New Orleans characters. From July 26 to August 17, 1922, Saxon published twenty short articles containing between 500 to 1200 words each, that were simply personality profiles. The name of the series implies that the articles were about unusual jobs, but instead, Saxon chose to report on unusual people. *Unusual Ways* was far more successful than *Choosing a Vocation* in making the reader empathize with, or at least understand the subject of the interview. This again highlights how Saxon's writing skills in character development improved with practice.

Biographer James W. Thomas notes that Saxon probably viewed these character sketch articles as mundane and were potentially among the reasons why the author quit *The Times-Picayune* in 1926 prior to moving to New York.[26] This is undoubtedly a correct assessment of Saxon's views. However, these brief articles required Saxon to practice and re-practice his skills of portraiture and character development in a sort of "wax-on, wax-off" exercise from which his writing benefitted. In fact, the characters about whom he wrote in these short pieces were often more convincing than those created in his longer works of this period, perhaps because the need for brevity forced Saxon to focus on the essentials while avoiding "too much fluidity."[27] These pieces comprise a sketch pad filled with the observation and practice necessary for the cleaner character development in his later speculative writings.

The historical record contains some additional information on the subjects in these stories; an editor's note after each story provides this background where it is available. Interestingly, many of the subjects of the *Unusual Ways* stories are first-generation immigrants and Saxon shows that this period in New Orleans was enriched by the cultures behind these new faces.

~

As a native New Orleanian, I was always aware of Lyle Saxon's role as a guardian of the city's history and architecture. But I began to study him in greater depth while researching the life of Charles Whitfield Richards, a New Orleans artist and journalist, for an upcoming biography that I am completing. The more time I spent reading Saxon's works, the more compelled I was to study his origins and earliest publications. While editing the text of the stories in this volume, I corrected obvious typographical errors, but left some quirky spellings unchanged (for example, "Sazarac" instead of "Sazerac," and "ginn-fizz" instead of "gin-fizz") in order to retain the flavor of the original work.

This year, 2018, is the tricentennial of the founding of the city by Jean Baptiste Le Moyne de Bienville, and 2019 will be the centennial of the conflagration at the French Opera and the bicentennial of the construction of the Pontalba Buildings. Reading some re-discovered writings of the patron saint of literary New Orleans is certainly a fitting way to acknowledge these milestones.

Michael Warner
September 2018

SHORT STORIES

1

WHO WOULD HUNT FOR SPANISH DOUBLOONS AND PIECES OF EIGHT?

Secret of World Roamer Still Secret Despite Key

Story of Man Found Dying on Sand Dune on Gulf Coast, and of Lure of Buried Treasure That Will Not Down—Map of Island in Caribbean Sea Unmarked by Either Latitude or Longitude—Entries in Diary.

Lately the newspapers have been full of stories of buried treasure, Spanish doubloons, pieces of eight. And, once again, I have delved into a long-locked chest and have taken out the map of that treasure island in the Caribbean sea.

Spreading the map upon the table under the lamp, I have gone over it, inch by inch—and once again the lure of that treasure is upon me. And yet, six years ago, I locked that map away, declaring it was all nonsense and madness.

I should have burned that map then; I don't know why I didn't—for as long as the map is in existence I shall have no rest.

The map, and the little black leather-bound diary came into my possession in a strange way, a way almost strange as the things written there.

Some years ago I taught school for a short time on the Florida coast, some sixty miles or more east of Pensacola. It was a small school, despite its high sounding name—and the big white frame building which seemed so imposing from the wharf, was little more than a barn when one crossed the threshold. The lower floor had never been finished at all, and the earth shoved between the sills. The stairs which led to the upper floor had no handrail—and it was a miracle that some of the children were not killed in their swift descent at recess time.

The schoolroom itself, which covered half of the second floor, had windows on three sides, and the walls were neatly finished; but above our heads the rafters showed, and when the wind came from the Gulf it made a strange singing sound through the great shell of a building.

The front windows looked out upon the sound—and a mile out there was a long, low-lying island, all pine trees and sand dunes. On very clear days from the school windows, one could see across the island, and catch a glimpse of the Gulf beyond, shining blue and clear to the horizon. There was something fascinating about that island and its sand-submerged trees—and I had always planned to go there, but week after week slipped by, and I did not go.

The other windows of the school room presented only a view of the thick pine woods—and the trees grew so close that they almost brushed the walls. I used to stand at the front window, in the morning, watching the children as they came to school in their motorboats—for none of them lived very near, and walking through the deep white sand was difficult.

There were only fifteen pupils in all, and they ranged from ten to sixteen years of age. Five of them were from one family, two from another, three from another. They were a quiet, hard working lot, and gave no trouble; they came to school, recited their lessons, and went home again.

I lived at a "hotel" some three miles away, and came to school, like the pupils, in a motorboat with one of my pupils, the son of the owner of the little hostelry. In the summer, the boy said, there were many guests, who stayed for two months or longer, fishing, bathing and resting; but in the winter I was alone there, except for the hotel-keeper, his wife and his son.

It was a strange life; and the children were strangely uncommunicative. I was only a substitute teacher anyway—only destined to stay for a month, and they felt little interest in me—or if they had interest, they did not show it. They were always polite, always studied —but when I tried to approach them on a friendly basis they became silent, and responded in short answers: "No, Professor," or "Yes, Professor," was all I could get from them.

One afternoon, when work was over for the day, I remained in the school room. The children had all gone. Guy, the hotel owner's son, had business to transact at the store, some miles up Santa Rosa Sound, and he had said that he would stop for me on his way home. After the last of the children had left the little wharf, and the popping sound of the motor boats had died away, I walked to the window and stood looking out.

It was a winter afternoon, and the sun was shining on the island with its clear radiance. As I stood, looking at the expanse of white sand, my attention was attracted by a flutter of something white—I looked again. It was too large for a bird's wing. The longer I looked, the more my interest grew; it appeared to be a flag of distress.

That flapping bit of white intrigued my imagination: I could not put my mind upon the neatly folded spelling papers which lay on my desk. I kept returning again and again to the window for a glimpse of that signal.

When Guy returned an hour later, I asked him to take me to the island in his boat. He betrayed neither surprise nor interest when I told him about the flag, nor did he hazard an opinion. So I did not press the matter. But, obediently enough, he brought his little purring boat close to the beach of the island.

"Can't go any nearer," he explained. "We're nearly aground now."

I looked down into the clear water. Sure enough, the white sand showed directly below the boat's keel. I removed my shoes and hose, and, gingerly enough, put one leg into the water.

The boy sat looking at me but betraying no interest. He had refused to go with me on my quest. I think that I should have turned back then, but the flutter of that little white rag, high on a pole, some distance inland was too much for my curiosity.

"Wait for me!" I said, and stepped overboard.

The water was deeper than I thought, and I stood nearly waist deep as I left the boat. It was cold, but I was determined. Something like a cynic's smile curved the boy's lips as I waded slowly ashore.

At the edge of the beach, I called, but there was no answer, and I went on. The ground rose sharply, and the sand ran between my toes and I climbed upward, clinging to bits of pine branches which appeared at intervals in the shifting sand.

At the top of the dune, I came to the sapling which held the signal flag. The flag was a man's white shirt, badly torn, and very dirty, but it flapped bravely. Still, no sign of a human being. I crossed the top of the dune and began the descent toward the other side of the island.

In a level space, under a small tree, a rude shelter had been erected, by simple expedient of fastening a piece of canvas over a bent sapling. A fire was smouldering nearby.

I called again.

This time a groan answered me, and I walked over and peered under the sheltering canvas.

A man lay there, disheveled, dirty. His face was covered by a month's growth of beard. His feet were bare, and only a pair of old trousers covered him. His shirt had gone to make the signal. His eyes looked out from shaggy brows, and were burning with fever.

How he got there I never found out—nor why he was hiding there; it was obvious that he was hiding, for a row boat and oars, pulled carefully upon the beach showed that he could have reached the mainland, if he had so desired.

It was easy to see he was dying, for death was stamped on his face.

I ran back and called to Guy, who sat stoically in the boat.

Together, we lifted the man and carried him over the sand dune, down to the motor boat. His eyes were glazed, but he kept tight hold upon a little packet he had thrust into his belt. It was a small packet, wrapped in oil-skin.

When, hours afterward, at the hotel a doctor came, he shook his head; the man was dying, he said. There was nothing that could be done.

The hotel-keeper, his wife and his son, were equally indifferent. It was a pity, they said, but what could they do? I sat by the man, wondering who he was, and thinking how dreadful that he should die like this, unknown, uncared for by those he knew.

Toward morning, just as the first faint light was greying the windows, the man roused and asked for a drink. I handed him a glass of water, but he pushed it aside.

"No, it's whisky I want," he said. It was his first intelligible phrase. I found some for him in the dining room and returned. He seemed better after he drank it.

For a few moments we talked—I asked him if there were friends that he wished to communicate with, or if there were letters to be written. He shook his head. There was nobody, he said, that would care a d—n.

After that he slept a little, and when the morning coffee came, he roused again, and talked to me. He realized that he was dying, and attempted to joke about it. But he was leaving me a legacy—yes indeed—a buried treasure!

He became serious. Well, why not tell me about it? I seemed to be a good fellow—I might get the benefits that he was missing. If I would only go to the island—and it was all so simple—I could find it all: Spanish doubloons, pieces of eight!

I must have smiled, for he became irritated. He swore. I didn't have to believe him unless I wanted to. I could go to h—l!"

I apologized. Later he went on with his story. He had been shipwrecked, he said, and he had found the treasure. He had stumbled upon it by accident: it was under a heavy stone, in a little cave. A vast treasure, vast! He had carried away a few gold pieces for proof, but they were gone now. He had been afraid to tell the man who rescued him about the treasure, for fear he would be murdered. He had planned to go back later.

But it had been difficult. There was no one he could trust. And then, after a voyage to China, he had gotten into trouble about a woman, he said. A man had been killed. And he had gone into hiding. He would tell me more later in the afternoon. He thought he could sleep now.

And so I went to school, as usual, that day, leaving the man with the keeper of the hotel. It was only after I had left the landing in the boat that I remembered the man had not told me his name.

I don't think that the children learned much that day; I was tired, distrait. I kept wondering about the man's sanity, and about his truthfulness. I thought of a hundred questions to ask him upon my return. But those questions were destined never to be asked.

The man was dead when I came home in the afternoon, and the coroner had been notified. Late that night his body was taken away. I never heard of him again. But the little diary and the map were in my pocket; he had given them to me—and no one claimed them.

I have kept them ever since, and have often wondered just what is hidden there.

There are no indications as to latitude and longitude on the map; all I know is that the island is somewhere in the Caribbean sea. It is a large island, some twenty miles long and half as wide. And it is almost bisected by a large stream which gushes from a hole in the rock, near one side of the island. The island was uninhabited.

The map is very clearly drawn, and is very explicit. Complete directions for approaching in a boat are given—and directions for penetrating the heavy undergrowth are explained in full.

But it is the diary which interests me even more than the island does. He was so intent upon that diary. It explained everything, he said. If I only puzzled long enough, it would come to me like a flash. I was not to worry about the verses, songs and bits of philosophy that he had written in, he said. They were all copied from books he had read, or from songs he had heard—just things which had interested him. But the other entries—those were the things which told it all. It was a complete record of his life and voyages, he said, for more than two years.

Oh, how I studied that diary! I took it with me when I returned to Louisiana, and I have had it ever since. I have read it over and over, time after time. But I know as little now, as when I began.

Some things are repeated many times: "Flight's Fancy" for instance, appears on every page in the book—sometimes twice or three times on a page. Does this mean, I wonder, that he has "moved on," that he has gone on his way? Or is it some phrase of the underworld?

One thing is certain, the man was obsessed with cards, wine and women. References to cards are numerous, and a dozen different women flit through the pages: "Ace High Baby," "The Virgin at the Blue Goose," and "Golden Doll."

You can read whatever you please into these scattered notes. but the thing fascinates. I have read it again and again—sometimes I almost believe that I have deciphered it—and then, just when I am almost upon the solution, the thing dissolves into thin air.

So I am putting those entries down here—just as they are written. There are no changes, no attempts at explanations. You must take them as they are. But if you have an explanation to offer tell me about it—and then, perhaps, I shall let you go with me, when we sail into the Caribbean, in search of the buried treasure.

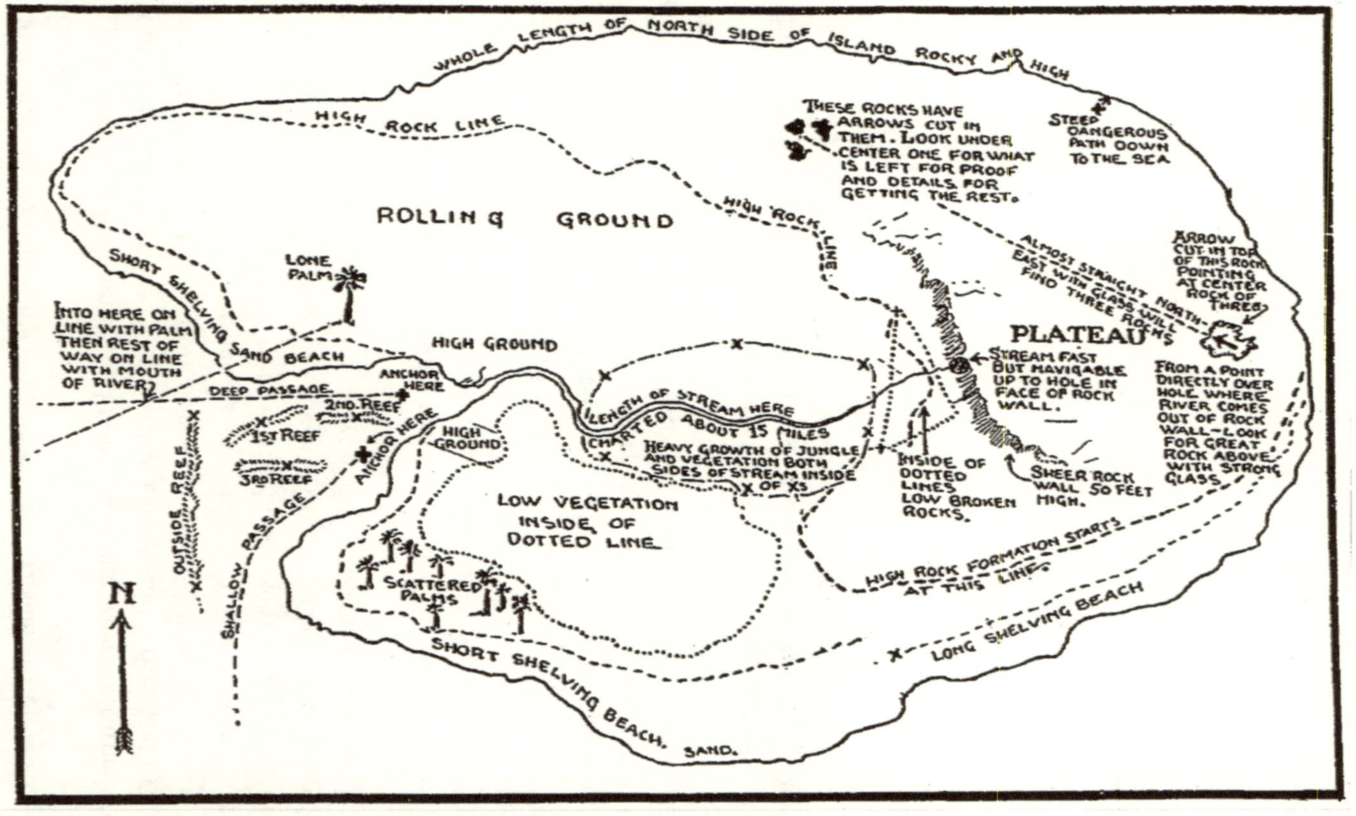
WHOLE LENGTH OF NORTH SIDE OF ISLAND ROCKY AND HIGH
HIGH ROCK LINE
THESE ROCKS HAVE ARROWS CUT IN THEM. LOOK UNDER CENTER ONE FOR WHAT IS LEFT FOR PROOF AND DETAILS FOR GETTING THE REST.
STEEP DANGEROUS PATH DOWN TO THE SEA
ROLLING GROUND
HIGH ROCK LINE
ALMOST STRAIGHT NORTH-EAST WITH GLASS WILL FIND THREE ROCKS
ARROW CUT IN TOP OF THIS ROCK POINTING AT CENTER ROCK OF THREE
SHORT SHELVING SAND BEACH
LONE PALM
INTO HERE ON LINE WITH PALM THEN REST OF WAY ON LINE WITH MOUTH OF RIVER?
HIGH GROUND
PLATEAU
STREAM FAST BUT NAVIGABLE UP TO HOLE IN FACE OF ROCK WALL.
FROM A POINT DIRECTLY OVER HOLE WHERE RIVER COMES OUT OF ROCK WALL-LOOK FOR GREAT ROCK ABOVE WITH STRONG GLASS.
ANCHOR HERE
DEEP PASSAGE
2ND. REEF
1ST REEF
3RD REEF
ANCHOR HERE
HIGH GROUND
LENGTH OF STREAM HERE
CHARTED ABOUT 15 MILES
HEAVY GROWTH OF JUNGLE AND VEGETATION BOTH SIDES OF STREAM INSIDE OF XS
INSIDE OF DOTTED LINES LOW BROKEN ROCKS.
SHEER ROCK WALL 50 FEET HIGH.
OUTSIDE REEF
SHALLOW PASSAGE
LOW VEGETATION INSIDE OF DOTTED LINE
SCATTERED PALMS
HIGH ROCK FORMATION STARTS AT THIS LINE.
N
LONG SHELVING BEACH
SHORT SHELVING BEACH. SAND.

Here is the Diary Left by a World Wanderer

This diary is written in a sort of cipher—or rather in terms which make it understood by few. Perhaps some of the words and phrases are familiar terms in "sporting" circles. It is evident that narcotics, alcohol and cards play a great part in his life; nor are the women forgotten. It must be remembered that this diary covers a period of two years or more, and it was written in many parts of the world. The last entries were made on the island where the man was found dying. The diary is given as it was written, only the poems and songs are omitted, and some obscene words are left out. It may mean nothing —or everything. The dying man said that the secret of the treasure was explained in it. Be that as it may, it is interesting as a human document. You can read into it what you please.

January: Flight's Fancy—500—Favorite. Three straights. Jack o' Hearts. One flutter—broke. Lealoah!

Meddling Miss at Panama.

Hole in the wall—Slide in, slide out - No quarter.

Black Bayou—Kum Bak—Nothing doing, bum steer.

Busted up—Golden flush—Got to howling. Never again!

Wistful Miss O'Chocktaw Bayou—In the Devil's Swamp. Hard luck.

Schooner Champion, 60 foot channel—B. S. L. Mississippi Sound —Gulf—Rigolets—First reach, second reach. Lake P. North Basin.

White Cloud. "Two sticker." Fast.

Everything gone in the flood. Hard luck but good losers. Jordan River. Flight's Fancy.

Oakdale, Mississippi. Some joint. Williams Camp, Edwards both rotten. 'Cadian girls pretty as pictures. Pine Hall, d—n lonesome.

Missed the ghost. Sorry. Virginia G: she fell hard.

Flight's Fancy. For a bone ring. A fool there was.

He fell again. Leaving for good. Bum town, bum.

On the third Palm Key. A chance for a jinx. Struck it. Rode the right one. O h—l.

Alligators, no place for me. F. F.

Mosquitoes. In the swamp.

D. S. Once for luck. Once on a summer's night.

Rattlesnakes. Lots of booze. Heat. No breeze. A good one. He got it.

Stillwater and cascade. "Silent Brook No. 2."

Pluma. Seven to one. He fell again.

The Golden Doll.

Trail in the air for Spider. In answer to a fair maid's prayer.

Dead. Flyaway. No limit. On the Ace o' Hearts. M. McM.

Youth's Fancy.

Roof of the Wordsmill. Here's looking at you.

Sky High Baby. For the Virgin at the Blue Goose. All or nothing.

Our motto: "Flight's Fancy," we said.

Death Valley. His kum-bak.

Struck hard on a poor loser.

Monkey river. 10,000 evil smells.

Lonely Miss and Wistful.

On the Ace o' Spades. The purple idol. Loaded dice.

The Golden Doll again. Lost on a deuce and a pair of sixes. She took it. He knew the trail. They all lied.

Hole in the floor at the end of the road. Never again.

The silver bowl. Tiger eyes. Havana. George and two Chinese. Mexico and a Dancing Doll.

Done forever. Off from it. The idol's eye. Flight's Fancy.

Diamond trail that night. Lost on a pair of treys.

Moonlight. Silver heels. She fell for a fool and a gold ring.

The end of the road and the Purple Light Inn. Some d—n old ruin.

Ace High Baby. Just gone, otherwise sudden—that was close.

Black eyes, dainty feet, pretty faces, graceful figures. Our move Steve, let's go!

Sorry Steve. Goodbye!

Some doll.

Jolly Roger. Twenty-five footer all smashed on Jordan River. Leaving with the Firefly.

Knocked out at Logtown, and down with the fever six weeks.

Live Oak Hall—when the lights went out. (That's the secret!)

J. R. Baby. His choice. F. F.

H. H. Gloomy place—long black nights. Out in the flood, July 8.

Tree ladders—white face.

Surinami—h—l boat. Panama City, palms and flowers, Cortez, hot, hot. San M'Gil Mexican Island. British Honduras, bum place.

Dolly—Flight's Fancy.

(Here follows a long list of poems carefully copied, mostly toasts and love lyrics.)

He got it on the Ace o' Hearts. Flight's Fancy.

Jack o' Hearts. Flight's Fancy for me.

(Just here the man has written in pages and pages of cowboy songs, evidently written down as he heard them sung.)

Varno Passage. The three great stories of the world. The girl was right.

In the Temple of Wat-Sutat of the coiled python.

The big soft rug in the Mosque at Stamboul.

Nikko, St. Kilda Pier.

Papeete, Callas.

Tanjong Dock. Dragged an anchor 30 feet, some man!

Black mouth of Kar.

Great Bell of Nagoya. The trail of the Dog Star.

By the beard of the prophet, she was right!

Scrolls of gold. Flight's Fancy.

At the Yellow Mermaid. With a fair wind all day.

River of 10,000 evil smells again. Some river!

Flight's Fancy. Women without morals, men without honor, children without virtue, flowers without smell and birds without song. They were right. Flight's Fancy.

In on a good one, left for good.

Sign of the spy-glass. O h—l! Flights Fancy.

Stuck on the third Palm Key. Fair wind.

Riding the right hunch, with the black horse of the bush.

Correct, old timer, F. F. for mine.

Me old pal Lou, with the Rattlesnake crew. Hot days, no breeze, no booze, h—l of a place.

Seal of Confucius. Dead.

Two stickers. Fast.

On a mud bar. Never again.

Met Tango. O h—l!

The hunter's moon. "Evil Eye" and "Flies." Flight's Fancy.

With the "R. S." Crew. Happy days. Lots of booze, hot sun, no breeze. In a good one. He got it.

Stillwater and Cascade. Trail in the air.

Flyaway. Played no limit.

Here's looking at you.

Youth's Fancy. M. McL. again.

On the roof of the world. Flight's Fancy.

For the Virgin at the Yellow Mermaid.

Sky High Baby. All or nothing. She lost.

Heading out, three to go.

Death Valley, they said. Flight's Fancy.

His kum-bak.

She struck hard. A poor loser. Lovey Miss. Remember the Alamo.

A long chance to the River of 10,000 evil smells. Our motto: "Flight's Fancy."

As in the beginning. Flight's Fancy.

The bamboo skeleton. Loaded dice for the Golden Doll and Ace High Baby.

She took it. Lost in the shuffle. They all lied. Never again.

A long time dead. Our move again. Sorry. To the Ace High Baby

Black masked woman. Some doll. Oh you Doc. Me for the woods.

Sleeping sickness.

Rockaway—a real hidden house.

Trouble, long nights. Flight's Fancy.

For a long sweet kiss. Which way? Bonnie, wrong hunch.

Japan and China. Chinese water police. Two bombs and a black cross at the mast head. Typhoon. Flight's Fancy.

In the saddle 48 hours. With a smashed knee. Out of luck.

Out of the game. Three months in the north.

Headed out November 3rd. Flight's Fancy.

Ugly women. No place for me.

Balmy days again.

Back with the old crowd. She took it. Best ever. That's the secret. Easy days. Playing for a Royal. If they knew? That's the joke. Flight's Fancy.

Oceans o'booze and once for luck.

She learned. Flight's Fancy. That's the secret. It cost her more than money.

Older and wiser. He fell again. It don't pay. Leaving forever.

Once more in the gloomy night. After the ball. Flight's Fancy.

Again, again and again. Lucky, I'll say.

She got it. That's where. F. F. was lost.

We found it. Flight's Fancy.

Over the ridge. What for? That's the secret. He will laugh forever.

Too late. He knew, but he was too slow. F. F.

Dunes again, and the black pool of death. F. F. was found. Flight's Fancy.

THE LAST ENTRY is scrawled and the writer is evidently very weak. The rest is silence.

Times-Picayune Magazine Section, April 9, 1922, p. 3.

2

AN INTERLUDE

The night air was so still that the candle flames burned steadily upward in long spirals, although the table had been laid upon the terrace in the open air. All around them the tropical night wove its strange web of witchery and moonlight. Far off a mocking bird called at intervals. The man lighted his cigarette from one of the candles and smiled at the beautiful woman sitting opposite him.

His lips framed the whisper: "Dearest, you are very beautiful tonight."

She smiled in complete trust and understanding, then she fell into a reverie, her gaze lingering upon the moonlit garden beneath them.

He continued to gaze steadily upon her! Gradually his face changed. He seemed cruel and tired. He spoke in a low, resonant tone:

"Yes, you are beautiful, but I am tired of you. You are ever the same; your very beauty grows monotonous. The thing which drew me to you at first has become the heaviest chain. I am tired of you, do you hear? Tired. Why have I tied myself to you for all time to come? There are other women more beautiful—and you with your damned smiling silence are driving me insane—I have given you more happiness than you have ever known before. Let me go! Let me go!"

The woman did not turn her head; she still gazed over the garden which was alight with fireflies. And she still smiled.

Then the man's face changed again; pity came over it, then tenderness. He touched her hand, and she turned to him again. His lips framed the whisper: "Let us go in."

She smiled in assent and rose.

Then he led his wife, who was both deaf and dumb, into the house, and kissed her quietly as she passed into the darkened library.

Times-Picayune Sunday Magazine, May 20, 1923, p. 4.

3

THE FORGOTTEN CIGARETTE

The mother entered the room softly and closed the door. Far off, downstairs, she could hear the laughter of her friends, as they had their last highball before leaving for the opera. She approached the bed and looked down at the sleeping child, slowly her face softened and lost its look of cynical indifference; she became almost motherly. Looking around, almost as if afraid of being observed, she kissed the little boy who lay sleeping there.

It was then that she became aware of her cigarette, which she had lighted in the dining room, and which she still carried in her hand. She placed it upon the edge of the table beside her, and then she fell upon her knees beside the boy. She pressed quick kisses upon his forehead, flushed a little with sleep; she poured out little love words to his unheeding face. Then she jumped up and ran out of the room, moving her eyes furtively. "What a fool I am," she said aloud. She reached the dining room before the guests had finished their highballs and in time to have another herself.

An hour later, as she sat in boredom looking at the world's highest paid opera singers, her home burned and her child died crying miserably for her.

So she went to a sanitarium and took the long cure; in the spring she was quite well again. Aside from missing a season, all was as before.

Nevertheless, the child's death had saddened her and she gave up smoking as a sort of penance, which of course was useless, but which gave her a sort of martyred feeling. And besides, smoking was making her teeth yellow. From her martyrdom she took much pleasure.

Here is the moral, bumptious reader:

A little control of the feelings will keep life balanced; a display of emotion is in bad taste at any time.

Times-Picayune Sunday Magazine, May 20, 1923, p. 7.

4

REPRIEVED

Here is the death cell.

Its narrow door is barred with iron, set criss-cross; opposite is a small window, doubly barred. A cot, covered with a gray blanket, stands against a bare wall; there is a bucket for slops. That is all.

The prison odor is in the air; the smell of men, caged.

Upon the edge of his bed a man is sitting, twisting his fingers in and out. Dirty fingers, with uncut, blackened nails. In and out. Otherwise he is still. His head hangs forward upon his chest; his dark hair is unevenly cropped. You cannot see his eyes. His mouth is twisted with pain—a soft mouth, like a half-grown boy's, lips colorless now and mumbling. His uncut beard covers his face, giving it a strange, haggard look, like some old picture of a martyr in his death agony.

A torn shirt, old trousers, a pair of broken shoes. The shirt is open at the neck; his chest is exposed, covered with fine hairs, black against his pasty white skin. Around his neck a rosary is knotted, its blackened beads distinct against the moist flesh. Drops of perspiration, like tears, are upon his cheeks and forehead. A man in torture.

This is the day set for his execution. A priest has been here to offer consolation, but the condemned man seemed unconscious of his presence. He only mumbled and twisted his fingers—And the priest went away. Now a reprieve has come. Sixty more days of life for Angelo Guirlando, while doctors examine him. In order to decide upon his sanity and his responsibility for the murder which he has committed.

The key grates in the lock, and the door swings open upon protesting hinges.

"Somebody to see you, Angelo," says the jailor. And you step inside.

The condemned man does not glance up, but with a cringing movement of his shoulders he acknowledges your presence. Another one to torture him with questions. You try to talk with him. One or two futile sentences die upon your lips. He only moans a little and continues twisting his fingers in and out. He has never lifted his head.

And the jailor stands watching you, jangling his keys.

IT WAS THREE YEARS AGO, in a cobbler's shop in Rockford, Ill., that Angelo first heard of the Italian girls of Louisiana. His brother had made a trip South, and when he returned he brought with him a pretty, laughing girl whom he introduced as his wife.

"You ought to get married, Angelo," his brother said.

Seated on his bench, Angelo turned his eyes upon this girl. He was a simple fellow good natured and kind, but intense. He brooded. He had not found a girl to please him in Illinois. Perhaps in Louisiana —? The seed was sown.

And so he came to the strawberry fields of Tangipahoa. It was late in June when he arrived, and it was at a Fourth of July celebration that he met the girl he married. He had been brought to the party by a man, a friend he had made shortly after his arrival. He had become greatly interested in Angelo's mission. Girls? Sure! Plenty of them. His own sister-in-law, for example, was one.

And it was this girl that Angelo met that night. They were together in a country not unlike his native Italy; there was a full moon, and the soft warm breeze from the fields. His passion for this strange girl consumed him from the first. He looked at her with his large dark eyes.

Who can say what happened? Who can tell of the warm, sweet kisses, the marriage? Suffice to say that Angelo was radiantly happy. He felt that he could never do enough for the man who had brought it all about. Here was a friend indeed. And the man seemed equally pleased. He went to the train with them, when they left, to wish the couple good-bye and good luck.

And so Angelo returned to Illinois, back to his old work bench and his wife was given a home.

BUT HIS WIFE WAS UNHAPPY. Angelo could not understand why. He would come home from work, of an evening, and find her lying across the bed, crying bitterly. It almost drove him mad. And soon the girl was to become a mother. Why did she cry? She should be happy. So Angelo reasoned. Hadn't he given her everything that a husband could give a wife? Doubts began to rise in his mind. He persecuted her with jealous questions.

All day long he thought and thought. At night he would lie awake, while doubts and fears clouded his mind. He began to question his wife more and more, his passionate love turning into suspicion and jealousy.

He was sure that another had possessed her. Another man had held her in his arms before Angelo had come. His name?

And then the whole miserable story came out. The other man was his own brother-in-law, the man who had first brought the girl and Angelo together. Four days before her marriage, this man had lured her out into the strawberry patch at night. He had threatened her with a knife. And he had taken what he wanted.

And now the girl was about to become a mother. Who was the father of the child, Angelo, or the other?

The problem would give him no peace. He could not sleep.

Was it here, perhaps, that Angelo's mind passed across that flimsy bridge which connects the two worlds, the sane and the insane? Or was it his insanity which constructed the whole story? At any rate, life was hateful to him. There was only one thing in his heart. Kill! Kill!

And so Angelo began to save his money. Every penny he made was saved toward his vengeance. He would return to Tangipahoa, and he would kill the man.

And so it happened. He left his home and came South again. The man was still there, friendly, unsuspicious. Angelo went to see the family of his wife and he told them his story. They could not believe it. Impossible. They reasoned with Angelo, trying to persuade him to go home. And, with hate in his heart, Angelo pretended friendship with the man, and went about with him, questioning, smiling, trying to make up his mind whether or not this terrible thing was true.

Who can describe the mind torn with jealousy? Who can tell of his suffering. But somewhere in his disordered mind, the thought came to him to go back to his wife—and to leave all as it had been. To forget. He would try.

The other man, all unsuspicious, was with him. He accompanied him to the train, as he had done when Angelo and his wife had gone before. And, as the men shook hands, the friend said: "Don't forget to tell your wife—"

A great gust of rage clouded Angelo's mind. He sprung upon the other like a lion—and killed him.

THAT WAS EARLY IN 1922. The parish of Tangipahoa was in a turmoil. Six Italians were on trial for an atrocious murder. Public feeling ran high. All of them were convicted and sentenced to be hanged. Angelo's trial came soon after. He tried to tell his story. He tried to make his motives clear to the jury.

But the testimony of his wife was damning. She denied it all. Angelo was mad, she said. Nothing had ever happened between her and the other man. It was all a delusion of Angelo's jealousy. Yes, it was true that she had cried often. Why not? She realized she had married a crazy man, a man who tortured her with his jealousy and his unfounded suspicions. She denied that she had ever confessed to her husband. She said he was insane, and the court decided that Angelo must hang.

He had been in the Parish Prison in New Orleans for nearly a year. For awhile he seemed normal enough, brooding a little, but he would talk. He seemed scarcely to realize what was in store for him.

Only once did he show passion. His wife came to see him. She came through the corridors, carrying her child in her arms. She spoke to him, through the bars, while the jailor stood, preparing to open the heavy door of the cell.

When Angelo heard her voice, he raised his head. A look of repulsion spread over his face. He rose, screaming, quivering.

"Take the little bastard away," he shrieked, and fell upon the floor, raving, moaning, saliva flowing from his mouth. He was mad with rage, violent.

And then, one day not so long afterward, the death warrant was read to him. He listened, but he could not understand its significance at first. It took him nearly a week to understand. Then he became a creature of terror. Only one phrase was heard: "Help me! Help me!" And it is this phrase that he is still mumbling, the guards believe, although the words can be distinguished no longer.

Since that time the clouds have lowered in his mind. He no longer speaks. Nor does he move about, except to pace nervously back and forth in his cell, his head hanging upon his chest, his fingers twisting endlessly.

This was months ago. His hair has grown long, and his finger nails. He became filthy. He tore at his clothes sometimes, but the blackened rosary remained about his neck.

When it is necessary that he be bathed, he must be thrown down and scrubbed, as one might scrub a dog. He no longer asks for food. If it is put before him, he will eat, but that is all. He is indifferent to all things.

As the day of his execution approached, he shows no sign of change. The day arrives when he must leave the prison for Amite where the scaffold is waiting. He never lifted his head. Captain Rennyson had received no word of the reprieve and he had Angelo ready to leave. The rope which was to be used at Amite and the black cap were bundled up. Angelo and the sheriff receive the message that the reprieve has been granted. So the sheriff returned alone.

Angelo showed no interest. He gave no sign that he understood what had happened.

The reprieve was given in order that alienists have time to make a thorough investigation of his case, to ascertain whether or not he is sane.

THE JAILOR STANDS JANGLING his keys.

Over in a corner, his head hanging forward, Angelo sits wringing his fingers in and out. You cannot see his eyes. His mouth is twisted with pain.

You make another effort to speak to him:

"Angelo! Listen to me!" No sign of his hearing, only a cringing movement at the sound of his name.

"Angelo! Can't you understand? It's all over. Everything's all right. The doctors are going to send you into the country!"

You believe it as you say it. Surely no group of physicians will see an insane man hanged. You feel sure of it.

But Angelo has not heard. He still sits mumbling, his fingers twisting in and out.

You feel suddenly, that the man is no longer there. Only a caged animal remains: his man's mind is gone. Another reprieve has come to Angelo, a different reprieve— something from out there, from the sunlight which lies along the roofs, beyond the barred window.

Times-Picayune, May 20, 1923, sec. 1-B, p. 1

5

FINGERS IN THE DARK

The prison chapel.

Colored religious pictures seem strangely out of place on the somber gray walls. Doors covered with iron. A vast re-echoing room, divided in the center by an air shaft, also barred, through which comes a medley of sounds and smells: shouts, blurred by the distance; a mournful chant of negroes' voices from their cells on the floor below; the rattle of dishes from the room where the prisoners are having their supper; the clang of a heavy door closing somewhere. The smell of food is in the air, mixed with that other prison odor, the odor of men, caged.

Sunset outside the barred windows.

Beneath a picture of a tortured form upon a cross, a woman is sitting. She leans forward as she speaks, looking straight at you with a strange earnestness. Her eyes are green, like sea-washed jade, her hair is vivid gold; but there are lines around her eyes, deep lines at the corners of her tight-lipped mouth. As she talks, she clasps and unclasps her fingers on her lap. Here is a woman who has tasted the bitterness of life, who has known tense days and sleepless nights—yet, she has come through triumphant. For her the past holds no dread; it is finished.

But it is of the future that you wish her to speak—Grace Gardiner's future. Her story has been printed in newspapers the country over—this woman who has been a drug addict for fourteen years, but who has entered the Parish Prison voluntarily in order to break herself of the habit, because she realized that she is not a fit mother for her child, otherwise.

"In ten days I go out into the world again," she says. "I am cured. Everybody has been sympathetic; nearly everybody has been kind. It has given me courage—and I need courage now.

"It's like coming out of a horrible dream. I'm just waking up to the fact that life is worth living—Captain Rennyson has given me my chance. Just as he's given many others another chance. I'm going to make him proud of me—"

She was silent a moment, thinking, then she continued:

"You don't know, you can't know, what it means to be free of it all—all the hypocrisy, all the lying—all the horror that I've known. You can't choose your friends when you're mad for drugs. Oh, I've known the dark alleys and the back rooms of dirty saloons—I've been to those places, crying, mad for morphine, but never mind that now—

"My old friends, the users of drugs, are my bitterest enemies now. Those are the people who have robbed me for years—the drug peddlers—how they have squeezed the last cent from me, over and over again. And now, when I'm trying to begin my life again, they are waiting for me, watching me—sure that I'll go back to them again."

She is silent for a long time, and as you sit there with her, your mind turns to that other woman to whom you spoke last night.

IN THE DARKNESS fingers clutch at your sleeve.

"Hello, where you goin' in such a hurry?"

It is a woman's voice, and you peer through the shadows at her upturned face, chalky white in the gloom.

"No! Don't go away!" Then with a quick change of tone she

continues, whining. "For God's sake, mister, won't you give me a dollar? Only a dollar. I've got to have it. I've got to!"

A policeman turns the corner, swinging his club. The girl grasps your arm and whispers: "Let's go in here!"

We are standing near a door which leads into a hall; above it a dirty electric light bulb illuminates a dirtier sign: "Ladies' Entrance." You follow the girl down a damp passage. A moment later you are together in a booth, walled on three sides, closed on the fourth by a faded green curtain. It contains a table and four chairs, otherwise it is empty. Somewhere in the saloon adjoining an electric piano is jangling and banging. The girl adopts her professional manner of "a good fellow"—she hums a little with the music.

She appears to be a mere girl, little more than twenty; but she is thin and haggard. Her heavily rouged lips make a red blotch on her ghastly face; the paint on her cheeks is like a mask. Her eyes are sunken, her face twitches. No wonder she finds herself reduced to pleading for a pittance for her miserable body. A reek of cheap perfume surrounds her.

She is nervous under your steady gaze, and makes an effort to rouse you with her shop talk: "What's the matter, daddy, blue?"

You smile, and hand the dollar across the dirty table cloth. Only a woman mad for drugs would have clutched it so eagerly:

"What will you have," you ask. " 'M' or 'C'?"

At the familiar slang of a drug addict, she smiles in turn, "You want a shot?" she asks. "We can get it here, if Tony's anywhere around." And without waiting for a reply, she calls aloud: "Tony!"

You hear, beyond the swinging doors of the saloon, the name repeated: "Tony, May's callin' you!" In a moment a man sidles between the curtains. He eyes you suspiciously, then looks at the girl with a question in his black, ratlike eyes. One look at Tony is enough. He, too, is a victim of the stuff he sells.

The dollar changes hands, and the girl receives a small piece of paper, wrapped around the white powder. "Alright, May," says Tony, and he is gone.

In the hem of the girl's skirt is hidden the needle and the syringe.

She has whisked them out in a moment, and is mixing the powder with water in a teaspoon. It is a slow process but the girl is dexterous. In a moment she has lighted a match beneath the spoon in order to make the mixture warm; then the needle is plunged into the solution, and the syringe is filled. You watch with fascinated eyes.

A moment later she has clawed up her skirt. Her thin leg is encased in a silk stocking, rolled below the knee. She seems to have forgotten that you are there; her finger and thumb grasp the soft flesh and pull it up; the needle is driven in.

She draws her brows together in pain, but only for a moment. There is a little pause, then the needle is driven still further into her flesh. She presses the lever slowly, and the mixture is forced into her body.

From knee to hip, above the stocking, the skin is punctured with scores of little black spots, hardly larger than a pin point, but proof enough of many similar injections. The little spots are dark against the pasty white of her skin.

She shudders a little, takes out the needle, and pulls down her skirt. Then she carefully conceals the implement in the torn hem of her dress.

She smiles at you: "Sure you don't want a shot? There's some 'M' left."

You shake your head.

"Do you blow it or bang it?" asks May, which in the slang of the addict means: "Do you sniff cocaine, or do you take hypodermics of morphine?"

A newspaper is lying on the table between you. On the front page is the story of Mrs. Grace Gardiner's fight against morphine in the Parish Prison. You call May's attention to it, instead of answering.

In a moment her face is flaming with anger, a flood of obscene and profane words are burled at the pictured face on the newspaper:

"The b—!" she snarls, "she's raisin' hell, ain't she? All this publicity about dope. All the peddlers are scared now, and the stuff is getting' harder and harder to get. The price has gone up, too.

"An' all for nothin'. Do you think she'll be able to stay off it? Well,

I guess not. She'll be back in a week. I know her. She can't let it alone."

"You know her?" you say in some surprise.

"Sure I know her. I used to buy my stuff from the same man whom she bought from. And look what she did to him. He's gone to the penitentiary for selling it—and because she tipped him off. She's a stool pigeon, that's what she is. Well, she'll get what's coming to her, all right, all right!"

"What do you mean?" you ask.

"I mean just this, daddy, when she comes out, there will be lots of us that will be glad to give her enough of the stuff go get her to takin' it again. But when she's got the habit! Well! That's when we'll get her. There ain't a peddler in the city who will sell her a nickel's worth. She'll be in one hell of a fix then!"

The drug has taken effect. May is herself again. She begins to talk of other things, while you sit silent, watching her. But you are listening no longer, you are thinking of what the woman has said.

All the drug peddlers, all the drug addicts, banding themselves together to drag this poor woman down again. Theirs is the typical cry of all their kind: "You can't keep away from it. What's the use? You'll come back to it—and to us!"

Truly are they called "dope fiends." Souls in torment in the hell of their own making, their fingers are stretched out toward their victim. Fingers in the dark, waiting, clutching, ready to drag her down—to place her into a blacker, more pitiful hell than their own.

In the barred chapel of the Parish Prison, Mrs. Gardiner sits, looking at you with her jade-green eyes, a frown creasing her forehead:

"Yes, I know—They would give anything to get me started again. The drug peddlers have gotten thousands of dollars from me in the last few years—they'd like to get the rest I have or can get—and then, too, they want to justify themselves, to prove that I'm as bad and as weak as they are. I can't blame them exactly. They're not normal. Dope makes your mind diseased, just as it weakens your body."

And then she clenched her fists:

"But they won't get me back. I'm cured. I'm sure this time. You don't know what that means, after fourteen years in hell. I can't tell you how terrible the craving for morphine is. When I think of the people that I have been friendly with, when I think of the filthy places that I've gone to get the stuff—I could cry for shame.

But now it is all over. Soon I'll be free—soon I'll have my boy in my arms again—my baby—"

She made a great, sweeping gesture.

"I'm free now. They can't hurt me. I'm through."

But the fingers in the dark are waiting nevertheless.

Times-Picayune, May 27, 1923, sec. 1-B, p. 1.

6

WELL! HE'S MARRIED NOW

You know him of course, who does not?—the man with the long flowing hair and the dark, thick beard, the man who always dresses in white, wearing a rakish white cap and walking bare-foot through the streets of the city?

Otto A. Marti is his name—and guess what? He got married Thursday! Yes sir, he did. Married a widow, Mrs. Blanche Bertha Kissinger. It was a very exclusive wedding, held in St. Patrick's Church in Camp Street. Father Raymond Carra performed the ceremony, and completed the wedding party. Mr. Marti didn't make much preparation for the event; he did put on white canvas shoes, but he took them off right after the wedding because they hurt his feet.

And now Otto Marti and his bride are occupying a love nest in Carrollton, in Olive Street, to be exact—a real honeymoon cottage, with green plush cushions on the parlor chairs, pink walls, vases on pedestals and lace curtains at the windows. And they are as happy as birdies in a tree.

Formerly Marti lived in the Vieux Carré—the home of artists, writers and prophets. He lived in the rooming house of Miss Margaret Bernard at 722 St. Louis Street. And the other roomers say that he has been anticipating this great and glorious day for many weeks.

Some weeks ago, upon a moonlight night, they were awakened by someone beating upon tin wash tubs in the courtyard. Angry heads popped out of windows. There, in the bright moonlight, Otto Marti was playing the drum upon two large zinc wash tubs, first a merry tattoo on one, then a rousing rattle upon the other. When asked the reason for this nocturnal outburst, he said that he was getting married soon—and this was an expression of joy.

And now, in the new love nest in Carrollton, he is happy indeed!

You arrive in midafternoon and knock upon the door. The new Mrs. Marti opens it for you and invites you in. No, she wants no publicity for herself, because her "folks didn't care for Otto"—and that's that. But Mr. Marti is willing to be interviewed. Yes indeed. Ordinarily, he says, he will not allow any paper to print any story about him—or even use his name for less than $8000—but this is different. You are welcome to every word he says today. This is a gala day. And it is a good day to speak of his future.

For Otto Marti is a man of boundless ambitions. You bet. He is the self-confessed head of the "Independent Americanism Party" and he intends to be the next president of the United States in 1924. It's a fact. He is also a prophet.

The afternoon was warm, so Mr. Marti had caught up his long hair into a neat chignon upon the top of his head—but his beard was flowing free. As he talked he puffed at a cigarette. A new and shining wedding ring glittered upon the third finger. The new Mrs. Marti also sports a new wedding ring.

"You know, I used to be a cripple," said the prophet, as he exhaled a cloud of smoke. "I couldn't walk without limping. But once, when I was going through Lafayette Square, a man spoke to me: 'Samson,' he called me. I wondered why, so I asked him. He told me to read the Bible, the Book of Judges, and after reading the thirteenth and fifteenth chapter I decided to let my hair grow long. So I did. Well, it cured me. I was no longer a cripple!

"Then the world war came long, and I was drafted into service.

They gave me a regulation army hair cut, and automatically I became crippled again. So they discharged me as unfit for service. I let my hair grow again—and got well immediately. But I never wear shoes, because they hurt my feet. The minute I cut my hair, I'll become a cripple again. Like Samson in the Bible."

Hastily you glance at the new Mrs. Marti, who is sitting quietly upon a settee, looking at you as you make notes. Suppose, you think to yourself, she should find that she was the reincarnation of Delilah. Armed with the shears, some dark night—

But your thoughts are interrupted by Mr. Marti's voice continuing his discourse:

"When I was a little boy, sweeping off the sidewalk in front of my mother's house, people used to stop me and ask me how to get cured of certain ailments. So I used to ask my mother how to cure them. Later on, I became a drug clerk, working for the Alco Drug Company, which is now out of existence. After six years, I lost my interest in drugs, and decided to be a healer—you know, all the saints and prophets in the Bible are able to heal the lame, the halt and the blind."

The implication of this is too much for you—so you sit silent, industriously scribbling down your notes, while Mr. Marti continues:

"Yes, I owe all my healing power to the Bible study—and I'm a sketcher, too. Wait. I'll show you some of my work."

He rises and goes into another room, returning presently with a series of paintings in water color which are as "advanced" as anything that the futurists ever did. They are very "elemental"—as the art critics say.

"Now this one," said Mr. Marti, "is a painting of a Frenchman. I call it 'Parlez Vous," and this is a portrait of myself, copied from a photograph of myself when I was eighteen, but I have added a beard and long hair!"

You write this down in your notebook.

"I am 34 years old!" says the artist, rather unexpectedly.

"Otto has lots of patients," said the bride from the settee, "Lots of people have been here today to buy his prayers. And he cures sick people, too."

"Yes, I'm in the doctor business," says Marti, stroking his long beard into submission and crossing his bare feet one over the other.

"Do you make much money in 'healing'?" you ask.

"Plenty to get along on," says Marti cryptically, looking down at the "prayer" he holds in his hands.

Mr. Marti sells the "prayer" for ten cents, and it is guaranteed to protect from burning or drowning, "nor will poison have effect on him" who wears it.

So, as you leave the love nest of the Martis, you carry away a "prayer" with you. Reading it, on the street car, you find out that:

"When a woman has labor pains, let her read this prayer, or let it be read to her, or let her wear it, and she will immediately be delivered, and when the child is born, let her place this prayer on the right side of the child and it will be safely preserved of eighty-two accidents. Whoever carries this prayer will never have any epileptic attacks, and if you see anyone having fits, place the prayer on his right side and he will be cured immediately."

You fold up the prayer: "Really, this is too much for ten cents," you say to yourself, "I ought to return it."

Down at the bottom of the page there is Mr. Marti's political announcement of his presidency in 1924. For ten dollars, he will sell you the use of his platform for gaining electoral votes for any office other than president!

So there you are!

Times-Picayune, June 24, 1923, sec. 1-B, p. 1.

7

THE LAST REUNION

The room is large and bare. The long lines of rough board tables stretch out from near the doorways into the darker recesses of the building; a clatter of dishes is heard as the negroes gather up the spoiled plates and cups and pile them upon trays. Upon the cement floor wet sawdust is strewn. Dinner is over. The veterans have been fed.

The temporary canteen established by the New Orleans Chapter of the American Red Cross is feeding hundreds of aged Confederates each day of the reunion in the vast and echoing structure at Girod and Magazine streets. And when the meals are over the veterans draw their chairs together to talk, to rest—or merely to sit in peace, rather than walk about upon the hard asphalt of the city's streets.

For they are no longer robust, these boys of '61, no longer strong and active. And it is good to be quiet for a while. Reunions are sad, nowadays, they say, for the thin gray line is diminishing, slowly but steadily.

Standing just inside the doorway, you look about. The picture before you is in tones of gray. Gray uniforms, gray hair, beards and bushy eyebrows; hunched shoulders, no longer able to stiffen for salute; palsied hands, sad old eyes which seem to look at life through a film of unshed tears. And they sit quietly, listening, it seems, to voices unheard by younger ears.

Capable girls and matrons, wearing the badge of the Red Cross, bustle about in the crowd, answering a question here, giving directions there. And in little groups the old men sit, talking quietly, or listening.

One is sitting alone. He is very old and feeble. His long white hair falls upon his shoulders and his soft white beard is scrupulously clean: his uniform is patched but neat, and he leans forward, his arms folded about two well-worn crutches, regarding you with faded blue eyes.

"Have you seen Duff?" he inquires. "I'm looking for him. I've waited a long time. All day yesterday, all day today. But he ain't come yet."

His tone is plaintive, child-like, wistful, but he smiles at you nevertheless, for his 80 years have taught him patience.

You reply that you do not know his friend, but that you will try to find him.

" 'Tain't much use, I expect," the old veteran continues, "he promised to come. He said he was comin' and he ain't never broke his word before. And I've known him for a long time. He's one of the oldest friends I've got, but I don't see him often, only at these here reunions. That's why I come to this one. Only, I'm afraid he's got disgusted and gone home."

"But why?" you ask. "Aren't you being treated right?"

"Oh, I ain't complaining," he answered, "but it feels kind of strange being here and not knowing nobody, not a soul and not being able to find your friends. I had a hard time finding my way here, but I'm all right now, I guess. The woman I'm staying with treats me just like a baby, but she means well enough, I reckon, and I appreciate it.

"And then, they are feeding us here and that don't cost us nothin'. I didn't know about this place until yesterday, or I'd been here before. I didn't eat much the first day I got here because I didn't have any money. You see, I ain't very well fixed for much at home, and so I brought along enough vittles to last me, I thought, all during the reunion. But Lord! They soured on me! Shucks! It's hot, you know, and I came a long ways all the way from Alabama. I live out in the country, near Jasper."

There was a pause and groups of the old men rise and go toward the door. One old man, with straight chin whiskers and a jelly red face, begins a speech addressed to the empty benches, while surprised-looking negroes pause in their work among the dishes to listen in wonder to this aged after-dinner speaker:

"Yes, ladies and gentlemen," the old man cries, tapping the floor with his cane, "I ain't got no kick coming, I tell you. If you don't take care of yourself in the city, well, who's going to take care of you, I want to know? I've been treated right!"

A chorus of taunts came from the old veterans around him.

"Hey, old man, you're blind! You ain't talking to nobody—only to empty chairs! Turn around this way." The old gentleman blinks and turns around, not at all abashed.

"Now, you boys is laughing at me!" he says. "But as I was sayin'," and he describes a gesture with his arm. "I've been treated right, down here in New Orleans. Oh, yes, I've heard some complaints, but I get along all right, and I 'spect the others could if they had any gumption about 'em! After every reunion you always hear a lot of kicks about the treatment the veterans get. But there's nothin' to it! I've been treated right and so I say—God Bless you all!"

He finishes with a gesture. One or two of his comrades laugh; others pay no attention.

One old man, wearing a high-peaked blue cap, leans forward, his hand to his ear: "What's the matter with him?" he quavers. "Is he mad about something?"

Nobody answers, because the late speaker has entered into a debate with another veteran relative to a wonderful cure for asthma. "I tell you, it's the wonder of the age!" he declares, "and I invented it!"

But the veteran you have spoken of at first leans forward, leaning upon his crutches: "You're Major Burke, ain't you?"

The red-faced veteran answers, "Yes, I am, and who may you be?"

Names are exchanged and then the crippled veteran asks his

question: "You ain't seen a man named Duff, have you? I've been waiting for him."

"Duff? Duff?" the other shakes his white head slowly. "I can't recollect that I knows him." And he passes on.

The crippled veteran turns to you again: "Mister," he says, "I'm sure tired of waitin'. I've been sitting here, right here. I don't want to do nothing without my buddie. Well, we've been going to reunions together for years and years. It's all I come here for, really—and now I feel I might as well go back to Alabama if I can't find him!"

Another pause and then he continues: "Yes, sir. I was in the Sixteenth Alabama Regiment, Company F. And I was wounded four times. My folks are all dead now, and I just stay at home, out in the country from Jasper. But I never miss a reunion. I want to see my friends—and that's all the chance I get."

Other veterans pass by and to each the crippled man makes his appeal: "You ain't seen Duff, have you, Why I've been sitting here—"

Another veteran, sitting nearby, is reading a newspaper, holding it close to his eyes. Suddenly he turns around and addresses the crippled man:

"Who you waiting for, old feller?"

"Duff."

"Louder, I can't hear you. I'm deaf!" and he cups his hand to his ear.

"Duff! Dr. Duff!"

"Well, look here, he ain't coming here. Look at the paper. He's dead!"

The crippled veteran turns his pale old eyes to the other, not comprehending: "You say he ain't here?"

The other old man loses patience.

"I say he's dead! It's in the paper. He died yesterday in a rooming house."

"Dr. Duff is dead?" quavers the crippled veteran, still uncomprehending.

"Yes, dead!" the old man's voice has risen to a high-pitched shriek.

"Dead?"

"Here! It's in the paper."

The crippled veteran begins to understand. He crumples up in his chair, his hands shake so that his crutches go clattering to the cement floor. Finally he speaks with an unevenly-cracked voice: "And I've been sittin' here and waitin'—"

He cannot understand all at once, this old man, he is too broken, too old, too crushed with the burden of life. But finally he shakes his silvery head.

"It's a long ride on the train—way out west of Birmingham—and it takes a long time to get there—" Then with decision. "But I'm goin'—I ain't goin' to wait."

The deaf veteran with the gray beard and the blue-peaked cap hears part of this and queries:

"Ain't you going to wait for the parade tomorrow?

"Parade? Parade? What's a parade to me? I'm goin' home!"

His voice is choked and husky, and his old fingers tremble as they lift the crutches. He is upon his feet and he begins his slow progress toward the door. Those around him are unconscious of his plight. They do not know, and if they did, they, perhaps, would not understand.

No, he wants nothing, this poor, old man, only a little peace, only to be let alone. He has attended his last reunion and now he is going home.

Times Picayune, April 13, 1923, p. 1.

8

THE ONE THING

Fate's Cruel Prank Upon a Blind Girl

Love is the power that rules the universe; yet the spark of love is sometimes not strong enough to overcome the handicap of nature. This absorbing story is an actual happening, as related to Mr. Saxon by the unfortunate blind girl herself. It is an unusual tale of how the twisted threads of fate can sometimes wreak havoc with the lives of human beings.

~

It is odd, but the words which best described Emily all began with the letter "b." For Emily was bland and blonde and beautiful—really beautiful, with soft, wistful, red mouth, a clear cut profile and lustrous gold colored hair. But, unfortunately, there is another word which must be given in describing her—another word beginning with a "b." Emily was blind.

Her eyes were blue and fringed with dark lashes; they seemed fixed upon the distance, filmed with a daydream. One would never have known that those clear eyes were sightless.

She had been blind from birth. She had never known sunlight or moonlight or the sight of clouds banked high upon a sunset sky. Nor had she seen a rainbow. The thousands of things which the average person takes for granted were missing in Emily's life. She could not know color, although she had an idea of it, and talked of it a good deal.

A Heart of Music

Color, she said, corresponded with the different keys in music. She had heard a poet say so once, in a lecture, and after that she was quite sure she understood. For the girl was a musician; she played upon the piano and she sang.

Seated at the keyboard, she would transpose Chopin's "Waltz in C Sharp Major" from one key into another. "Now it is red," she would say. "Now it is green." She would play a few bars more, and then transpose the tune again. "Listen, don't you hear?" she would ask. "It is blue!"

Her sister Olive would listen and say that she could hear the color, too. But she was never sure. Sometimes she could not say whether the melody was yellow or red—and this annoyed Emily.

The sisters were poor. It had been a struggle for Olive to send Emily off to school, but she had done it, and Emily had emerged after eight years at the State School for the Blind, with a diploma in music, which was for her pleasure, and with a real ability to earn her living as a stenographer.

A Stenographer—and Blind!

In taking dictation, she used a little metal device which she called a "slate." It was covered with numerous perforations, and it was made in two pieces, one of which folded across the other. A piece of paper was put between the two sides, and the slate was folded up. Through the perforations Emily made little holes in the paper with a sharp needle; and she could read it afterward, with her finger-tips. The "Braille System," it was called.

Seated at her typewriter, she could take dictation direct to the machine. She did it rapidly and easily. There was never a temptation for her to look at the keyboard, as she could not have seen it had she looked. Therefore, she was never distracted from the task in hand. And she was a good stenographer.

She secured a position in an office, one of a number of girls employed—and she did her work better than most of the others, despite her sightless eyes. She worked for a group who did social work among the poor. Year after year she worked in the office.

Never a Mistake

When visitors would come in, her employer would take them up to Emily's desk and ask her to go through her tricks. For their edification she would write amazingly fast upon the typewriter, and would pull the paper from the machine and hand it to them, sure that there was not even one mistake. The visitors would exclaim and ask questions—and Emily would answer, smilingly.

She had always been blind; and she was not mawkishly sentimental about it. She realized her handicap, and she proceeded to go ahead with her life work as best she could. It was commonplace enough to her. But Emily was never commonplace to other people.

At home, sometimes, she would grumble a little to her sister: "It gets a little monotonous sometimes," she would say. "I get tired of being pointed out and sympathized with, and pitied."

An Envious Position

Then Olive would smile and say: "Well, perhaps you are luckier than you think. Nobody notices me at all. I work hard and work pretty well, but nobody pays the least attention. I might as well be a clock on the wall, or a calendar. I'm just one in a hundred, among the bookkeepers and clerks in our office. If I dropped out, I'd never be missed. You've got personality. Everybody notices you. If you had a snub nose and skimpy hair like mine, if you were ugly and 35 years old—and looked it—perhaps you wouldn't like it so much. Sometimes I believe I'd be willing to change places with you."

And Emily would say: "Am I really pretty? Are you sure that you are not telling me this to make my blindness a little easier to bear? You wouldn't do that, would you, Olive? It wouldn't be fair."

In their bedroom, at night, the girls often spoke of love and marriage. Emily was firm in her views.

Will He Ever Come?

"I'll never, never marry a blind man," she would say. "If a fine handsome man, a 'seeing person' would ask me—well, it would be different then; I'd like children, you know. If a real man would come along, somebody that would treat me just as an ordinary girl and not pity me or be maudlin about my blindness. But I'm afraid, Olive, that he'll never come."

Olive could follow her sister's thoughts. She knew that the other girl referred to those blind boys who came sometimes to their little apartment to see Emily—old friends from the school. Olive was not so sure that Emily was right in rejecting them.

"I don't see what difference it makes," she would say. "I don't see why you object to a blind man so much. Some of them are awfully nice, you know."

"Would you marry one?" Emily would retort. "I doubt it! Or, if you did, you could take care of him and guide him about. But I can't do that. No! I can't see anything in this 'blind leading the blind' sort of thing."

A Man Enters Her Life

One day Emily's employer read a letter aloud to her, asking her to answer it. The letter was from a music critic on a Boston paper. He wrote asking some information relative to music among the negroes of the city. He was writing an article on folk songs, he said, and he wished information. Her employer told Emily to answer the letter as she saw fit, and to sign her own name, so that any future correspondence could come direct to her.

Emily answered the letter at length. She was interested in the man in Boston, as his name was known to her through articles in musical journals which her sister read to her. And this was a subject that Emily knew a great deal about; negro music had always interested her.

That night she told Olive about it, and Olive shared her sister's interest in the music critic in Boston. She even found a picture of him in an old magazine, and she described him to Emily.

A week later his answer came. Such a friendly letter. He thanked Emily for her trouble in answering so fully, and he wrote a little about his own work. He ended by asking other questions—and Emily hastened to reply.

Music a Bond

A correspondence began. Twice a week one of his letters would arrive, and twice a week Emily would answer. They wrote of music, mostly, because that was a bond between them, and they wrote of the theater and concert. For the first time in her life, Emily knew the feeling of perfect equality. The man had no idea that she was blind, and he thought of her as any other girl. He treated her with a frank camaraderie which delighted her.

Olive was equally interested, for, of course, she knew all about him, and it was her duty to read and reread his letters aloud. And so it developed, gradually, that Emily fell in love. She was not quite sure of it herself, but Olive was positive and she cried a little at night, cried quietly into her pillow, for she was sure that her sister would be hurt. Once she tried to talk of this.

"You should tell him of your blindness," she said. "Suppose he should find out from someone else."

Just Amusing Himself

"Who could tell him?" Emily answered quickly. "I'm nobody. Nobody knows me. He's famous. He's only amusing himself, anyway. Do you suppose that a great man would waste his time with a silly little stenographer in a town a thousand miles away? Why, he must have hundreds of friends near him—No, Olive, I'll never tell him. I couldn't bear it. He'd change. He'd be sorry for me." A little sob came into her voice, "He'd call me 'a poor blind girl!' and all the rest. I'll never tell him. It would be horrible."

But all the same, Emily did not quite believe what she had said so glibly. For his letters were warm in their friendship. He was even a little tender sometimes, and Emily would smile to herself as she went through her routine in the office, for gradually this man of letters was taking all her thoughts. She was happier than she had ever been in her life, and she went about with a smile upon her lips, her head lifted.

Hides Her Blindness

She used to plan in every way to make him think that she was like other girls. She wrote every week of the concert she had attended and the plays that she "saw." For it was true; she did go often to the theater and the concert, always with Olive. At concerts she enjoyed herself even more than her sister, but in the theater, Olive was necessary in order that she could hear how the actors looked, what they wore and what they did. And, of course, moving pictures were nothing to her.

Whenever the man mentioned the moving pictures, Emily remained silent in her replies. But once she was in a dilemma. The man had read in the papers of a certain exhibition of modern paintings which was being shown in Emily's town, and he asked her opinion on one of them. The canvas had been painted by a friend of his, and he wanted to know what she thought of it.

Emily was in a panic. Olive tried to solve the problem by going to the exhibition and telling Emily about it. But Olive thought the picture was hideous, and found it too bizarre and she could make nothing of it.

Her First Lie

So Emily, for the first time, must lie. She wrote that she had been unable to attend the exhibition, because she had been ill. And, to distract his mind from the subject, she turned with renewed interest to descriptions of concerts and the theater.

"Aha?" the man wrote in his next letter. "So you don't like the moderns! I could read between the lines in your letter. You're being polite! Shame on you! Now, I'll make a confession. I don't like them either. In fact, I don't understand what they are trying to do. Now, in music, it is different. I think that Scriabine—" and on at length.

Both Emily and Olive sighed with relief when they realized that the dangerous moment had been avoided. "Better tell him the truth, Emily," Olive warned again. "Something will happen. Fate, you know."

But confession was too hard, and the man's friendship had become almost an obsession with the blind girl.

"I Won't Tell Him"

"I don't care what you say, Olive," she said, "I won't tell him. And, if I'm punished, I'll pay. But don't take this from me. It's the only thing I've ever had that I really wanted—this man's friendship, I mean."

Christmas was approaching. The shops were full of gifts, and all day long a stream of holiday shoppers filled the streets. Emily spent hours in knitting a muffler for the man in Boston. It was beautifully done, and Olive praised it highly. She selected the color, a soft gray, and Emily had struck "gray" chords on the piano, trying to visualize it. A week before Christmas it was sent away by parcel post. Emily and Olive had gone together to the post office, buffeted by the holiday crowds.

On Christmas Eve a package arrived from Boston. Olive had come home before Emily, and had found it lying on the table in the little hall of their apartment. She picked it up and stood holding it. What could it be? It was too heavy for jewelry, or a card case. Olive decided that it must be an ornament of some kind.

A Present for Emily

She sighed as she stood there, weighing the package in her gloved hand: "Oh, I hope it is something that Emily can enjoy," she said to herself. And she put it away carefully to keep until Christmas morning.

The next day was a holiday for both girls. A streak of sunlight came in at the window and fell upon the pillow of the blind girl. In her sleep she felt the warmth, and it awakened her. She smiled to herself. "It's a nice day," she said. "We can go for a walk."

She reached beneath her pillow and found her watch; by opening the case, and placing her fingers lightly upon the hands, she could tell that it was nearly 7 o'clock. This watch, made especially for blind persons, had been her sister's gift to her many Christmases ago.

She slipped quietly from her place and groped her way across the room until her fingers touched the cool brass rail at the foot of her sister's bed. Then she felt her way until her hand rested upon Olive's cheek.

"Merry Christmas!" she called, slipping her gift into the hand of the other girl.

Her Friends Remember

Together they opened the presents which were waiting. Books for Olive and other trifles; for Emily there were kind and thoughtful gifts: a bottle of her favorite perfume from her sister, a soft, wooly dressing gown from the girls in the office, two phonograph records from one of the boys who had been in her class at the school for the blind, a pair of knitted slippers from another blind girl, some Christmas cards, punctured by the Braille system and easily read with the fingers – these were from her friends she had known in her school days. Emily could feel the sharp, prickly leaves of the holly, and the silky ribbons and crinkly tissue paper which were strewn upon the bed.

"Is there anything else?" she asked.

One present remained. His present. Olive slipped it into the other girl's hand. Emily's face was alight, and her fingers tugged at the string which held the parcel. It seemed that she had never been so happy.

She opened a layer of paper and her fingers encountered a square of stiff paper: "A Christmas card?" she asked, trembling a little.

Olive opened it: "No, better than that—a letter."

"My Dear Little Girl"

"Quick, read it," said Emily, and stood there beside the bed, holding the package in her hands, still unopened. She was a little breathless now.

Olive slipped the crackling paper from its envelope:

"My dear little girl," she began. Then she paused in surprise: "You know, Emily, it sounds so—so personal," she said. "I don't feel that I should read it—"

Both girls laughed a little at the familiar joke between them, then Emily spoke:

"Please go on, Olive," she said. "He never wrote like that before—I never dreamed—" and then she broke off. There was no laughter in the eyes of the other girl, as she read; but her voice was calm as she continued:

" 'I am sending you the one thing that I am sure you will enjoy, and with it, all my love and good wishes for a merry Christmas.' "

"And is that all?" asked Emily.

"That's all, dear, and his name, of course—"

"The one thing that he is sure I will enjoy," said Emily slowly, her face was shining as her fingers tugged at the paper which wrapped the present.

Something tugged at Olive's heart, a vague warning, a premonition. She sat watching her sister as if fascinated.

The blind girl's fingers tore off the last wrappings, opened the box and fastened upon the object within. She seemed puzzled for a moment, and her fingers groped their way over the surfaces of the object which she held in her hands. Suddenly she uttered a low cry.

The thing fell from her hands upon the bed, where it lay, shining in the sunlight which came in at the window, sunlight which made the golden filigree and black enamel gleam strangely.

Yes, it was the one thing which symbolized the difference between the blind girl and the rest of the world, the one thing which made her a person apart, beyond the world of light and color and beauty.

And Olive, dumb before the irony of life, sat watching the sunlight glitter upon the gold trimmings of the opera glasses which lay there, slipping from their velvet case.

Times-Picayune Sunday Magazine, May 27, 1923, p. 1.

NEW ORLEANS HISTORY AND PRESERVATION

9

FRENCH OPERA HOUSE TO RISE AGAIN FROM RUINS

Last Ballet in Historic Old Place of Music—The Dance of the Flames

Fire Leaves Famous Home of Lyric Drama Great Heap of Ruins

Falling Walls Menace Many

~

Shrine of Merriment and Many Loves, Dear to Heart of Every Orleanian Known Throughout the World, Wrecked by Early Morning Blaze Which Leaves Nothing But Memories and Ashes.

The French Opera House burned early Thursday morning. Only the toppling walls remain, surrounding a heap of ruins. Gone is all the glory which has marked the building for more than half a century —gone in a blaze of burning gauze and tinsel, a blaze more splendid and more terrible than Walpurgis Night, that long-famous Brocken of the opera "Faust".

And into the hearts of the people of New Orleans there has come a great sorrow, a great mourning. For there are few women here who have not tendered memories of their vanished youth, their debutante days, loves, heartburnings, joys—all intimately linked with the French Opera. There are few men who have loved or been loved, who have not recollections of the nights when they sat in the dreamy darkness of the old building, listening to the voices of great singers blending with the orchestra, and thrilling at the touch of a bit of gauze, as it brushed their cheeks.

Children, taken to the opera with their mothers, learned their first lessons in art and music, while watching the singers upon the brilliantly lighted stage. Later, the girls as debutantes received homage as they sat in the horseshoe, surrounded by flowers, admiring and admired, loving and beloved. Still later, as matrons, they joined gay parties, listening to the same old operas, the same dear, cherished operas, sung by different voices, never losing their charm; here they watched their daughters and sons growing to love light and color and art as they had done, in the old Opera House.

Then, last of all, as old ladies they have come to see and hear, while their grandchildren have wandered about the foyer and the promenade chattering, laughing. The old are not so merry in their pleasures at the opera, but they return to it as to an old friend, to listen, to look and to enjoy. It seems like returning home. The opera is hallowed in their hearts; it belongs to them by right of years of possession. For in New Orleans and in New Orleans alone, is the opera so personal, so completely ours.

Gone, all gone. The curtain has fallen for the last time upon "Les Huguenots," long a favorite of the New Orleans public. The opera house has gone in a blaze of horror and of glory. There is a pall over the city; eyes are filled with tears and hearts are heavy. Old memories, tucked away in the dusty cobwebs of forgotten years, have come out like ghosts to dance in the last, ghastly Walpurgis ballet of flame.

The heart of the old French quarter has stopped beating.

Fire Does Work Well

The fire, which originated at 2:50 a.m. Thursday morning, did its work well. The entire structure was destroyed within a few hours.

The cause remains a mystery. Fire Marshal Haggerty and his assistants questioned a number of persons he thought possibly knew something about the origin of the blaze, but finally decided to postpone the investigation to Friday morning. A number of witnesses have been subpoenaed and a thorough investigation is promised.

The fact that there was no loss of life probably was due to the awakening of the young child of Mr. George Damon, whose husband is part proprietor of a restaurant on the ground floor of the building. The Damon family, which lives in four rooms just above the restaurant, was awakened by cries of the infant, who was almost smothered by the big volume of smoke pouring into the bedroom.

Wall Topples Over

After the flames had been burning several hours, during which time they tore out everything in the old building, a part of the Toulouse street wall fell, the debris crashing down upon the water tower of No. 2 fire company, and upon the undertaking establishment of Valoni & Bonnot, across the street. No one was injured.

According to the police, Ginlio Bramucci, concert master, and Mario Mazini, both members of the New Orleans Grand Opera Company, discovered the flames. While on their way to their rooms at about 2:50 a.m. Thursday they saw smoke issuing from windows on the second floor of the theater. The windows are just above the restaurant operated by Pletrodi Silvestri and George Damon.

Bramucci and Nazzoni ran to the saloon of John Arnstedt, Bourbon and St. Louis streets, and notified Arnstedt, who immediately telephoned the central fire station. An alarm, it is said, also was turned in by box 139 at 3 a.m. A general alarm was turned in shortly after.

According to William Niel, custodian of the opera building and who resided in the structure, there was a general rehearsal of the company Wednesday night. After the rehearsal was finished about 11:45 p.m., he said he made his rounds of the building and found everything right. He then "closed up" and retired, and knew nothing of the fire until awakened by persons he does not know.

Mr. and Mrs. Pietro di Silvestri, restaurant proprietors, retired at about 1 a. m. They were awakened, they said, by Mrs. Damon's baby, who, half-smothered by smoke pouring into the room, cried for his mother. Silvestri then went down into the restaurant and opened the doors in an endeavor to release the smoke.

Flames Break Through

Mrs. Silvestri, who had remained in her room, saw flames suddenly burst through the partition of her room, and she rushed downstairs to her husband, the couple then leaving the building.

According to Silvestri, as far as he knew there were no oil heaters on the place, and the kitchen of the restaurant was located in the yard, a few yards away from the building.

The French Opera building, which was owned by the Tulane Educational Fund, was carried on the fund's books as being valued at $47,000, but the actual value was estimated at $250,000. The fixtures, all of which are a total loss, were valued at $25,000. The building and fixtures were insured for $25,000 in the Milwaukee, Mechanics, National Underwriters, Stuyvesant and Jersey City fire insurance companies.

Louis P. Verance, impresario of the opera company, said Thursday that the musical scores, costumes, scenery—property of the opera company—and all wardrobes owned by the artists, valued at about $50,000, were a total loss and were not covered by insurance.

The three-story brick building at 826 Toulouse street, owned by Miss E. Halstre of Metairie Ridge, valued at about $25,000 was damaged about $1500, the amount of insurance carried being yet unknown. The ground floor of the building is occupied as an undertaking establishment by S. Valenti and Kames Bonnot; the second floor as a rooming house by Mrs. Raymond Delgado, and the third floor by Mrs. Joseph Livera.

The property of Valenti and Bonnot, valued at about $5500, suffered a damage of about $800. This is insured for $5600. Mrs. Delgado's property, valued at about $700, was damaged $300, with no insurance carried.

The wooden outhouse in the rear or the building at 513 Bourbon street, occupied by Salvadore Corniglia, suffered slight damage. The gallery of the house in the rear of the building located at 515 Bourbon street, occupied by Anatole Cresson, was also damaged slightly.

Water Tower No. 2, stationed at the Central Fire Station, valued at $11,500, was damaged about $5000 when the wall of the opera building fell on it.

Will Show Sunday

The New Orleans Opera Association expressed its sentiments in applause Thursday at noon when the association rallied to the emergency and completed arrangements for a gala reopening Saturday night at the Athenaeum. Arsene Perrilliat, president, has issued a summons for all directors to be present at the conference and the complete roster responded with the unanimous idea of continuing what has begun as one of the most successful seasons New Orleans ever has known.

Harry B. Loeb and Louis P. Verande, manager and impresario, were ready to produce the performances of "Palliasse" and "La Navarriase" as scheduled Thursday night, transferring them to the Athenaeum. They were backed in this plan by the entire troupe of singers and musicians. Officials of the opera company, however, persuaded them to postpone the performance, and insisted on cancelling the agreement for Thursday evening.

Tickets for the Saturday performance went on sale at once, and the performance of that night is being planned as a gala event when New Orleans expects to come up smiling after what is generally regarded as a unique calamity in the city's history.

Orders for new musical scores to be rushed from New York and other cities by express were issued by noon Thursday. As soon as the meeting at the Grunewald Hotel closed at 2 p.m., Mr. Loeb with Theodore Roehl and Mr. Verande, hurried to the Athenaeum to begin arrangements for Saturday night. Mr. Perrilliat declared Thursday the public need have no fear that the performance Saturday would be a "trumped-up affair."

Although there seems to be no doubt in the minds of members of the association that opera will continue as scheduled this season, the fate of the year's program will not be decided until a meeting Sunday at 10 a.m. at the Gurnewald Hotel.

Will Be Restored

The conference Thursday was devoted exclusively to plans for resuming work as soon as possible in other surroundings, but individually members expressed themselves as positive the French Opera House's restoration is a matter of only a short time.[28]

"If New Orleans in 1859 could build such a structure as the old opera building, what could we do today, with a population of almost half a million?" Mr. Perrilliat said. "When subscriptions are opened I believe the fund will be raised in several weeks."

Ernest Lee Jahncke strongly advocated a building combining an opera house with an auditorium.

No official action along these lines has been taken, but rumors of contributions pledged and others ready for the time of asking were circulating freely.

Attending the board of directors' meeting Thursday were Arsene Perrilliat, F.W. Evans, S.J. Shwartz, Ernest Lee Jahncke, A.S. Amer, Theodore Grunewald, Parham Werlein, W.R. Irby, I.D. Moore, Alcee Gelpi, E.V. Benjamin, T.J. Hill and L.P. Burthe.

Walls Dangerous

City Engineer T.L. Willis and City Architect E.A. Christy, inspected the ruins soon after the fire and found that the walls still standing were in a dangerous condition. Upon their advice the cars were diverted from Bourbon street and police precautions taken to keep vehicles and pedestrians away. Notice was sent to the Tulane educational board to tear down the walls at once.

By 9 o'clock Thursday morning the streets below Canal were filled with streams of persons heading for one point. It was not the usual crowd flocking to a fire from morbid curiosity, but composed of men and women of all stations and generations going to pay last tribute to the old opera's final moments. Business men, hearing the news on the way to offices, had hastened down as if to the assistance of an old friend in trouble. Women from the uptown residence districts came in automobiles, and Canal street store employees used the extra hour before opening Thursday morning to pay their respects to the smoking ruins. One woman with white hair had tears in her eyes as she leaned from the window of a limousine and gazed at the broken shell of the historic building.

"What memories for me the old opera always held!" she sighed. "Now they are gone with all the rest."

Persons stood about, oblivious of the drifting spray from the hoses still playing from all sides and the smoke of the engines. A young woman high in social circles parked her dashing red roadster in a side street and splashed through the streaming gutter to get a view. When she saw she fell back with a cry of dismay. A priest who has directed a parish in the old section for forty years, shook his head at her with a sigh of sympathy and at the same moment a husky young fellow in the uniform of the marines turned to them impetuously.

"Our opera house gone! Oh, why could it not a-been some other place?" he voiced the thoughts of all three.

Home Emptied

Residents of the neighborhood chattered in garbled tongues and depicted with eloquent hands the experiences of the night. Mounds of household goods stood at intervals along the street, guarded by women wrapped in shawls or by children still clad in costumes improvised when the alarm was given. Almost every dwelling in the danger zone along Bourbon and Toulouse had been emptied on the advice of the firemen, who feared at first the high wind might cause a spread of the flames. Tumbled bed clothes, furniture in all stages of use, garments, cooking utensils and pictures littered the banquettes.

On one great heap in Toulouse street a sort of impromptu shrine had been erected by placing a figure of the Virgin atop a pile of furniture. A wrinkled Italian woman, guarding the goods, chattered constantly and unintelligibly to a circle of awed listeners. She was explaining how the Virgin had saved her family from death when the outer wall on the Toulouse street side collapsed. The last brick of the ruin struck just at the edge of the heap of household belongings where the family huddled in terror. If the wall had swayed just half a foot further in its fall—!

Above the clouds a stream and smoke and the spray of the fire hose rising high in air there flashed hundreds of wings against the blue sky. Great numbers of pigeons, which have dwelt for years in the high nooks of the old building, were cast out upon the world. As if patiently seeking some relic of their homes they returned again and again to the jutting fragments, although driven out constantly by smoke and water.

Singers Hover About

In the street below the artists of the troupe behaved in a somewhat similar manner. With costumes, musical instruments, scenery and opera gone, they hovered in the neighborhood of the ruins. The happiest woman in New Orleans was Mlle. Lucien Lavedan, the harpist who was snatched from despair to delight within twenty minutes Thursday morning. She was mourning the loss of her glorious harp, said to be one of the finest instruments in America, and worth a small fortune. A fireman touched her on the arm.

"Miss was that thing you're talking about something like the insides of a piano stood on end?" Mademoiselle admitted that the instrument might bear some resemblance to this description.

"Well, there's a lot of wires strung on a gold thing sitting right down the street there."

Mademoiselle ran like the wind, and there, on the curbstone of Bourbon street, sat her treasure, its strings not even out of tune. It is said to be the only article of value rescued.

Opening Night Gay

Debutantes and dowagers are mourning the burning of the opera house, which has put a temporary halt to one of the most brilliant social seasons in the history of New Orleans opera. The opening night, when the debutantes formally "came out" in box or horseshoe, added another chapter to the record of the Crescent City for beautiful women and exquisite gowns. The foyer, with its new velvet curtains, of which Mr. Loeb was very proud, was more than ever a meeting place for the elite, its long mirrors reflecting scores of coquettish smiles, tulle creations and aristocratic back-bones. A custom much in vogue this season was that of general visiting, unheard of in grandmother's heyday, when only the men flitted like butterflies from box to box and it would have been considered shockingly improper for a girl to do anything but sit still and smile.

The opera house will be missed far more by older people than by debutantes. Old ladies with diamond necklaces to exhibit as they languidly "rubber" through their lorgnettes will long for the gentle play of the footlights on their boxes more than the sweet young things, who find as much pleasure in dancing to jazz as in listening to "Faust." And to the middle-aged couples who enjoyed a chat with their friends in the scene of their youthful pleasures as well as to the real music lovers of the city, the passing of the opera season will be a real loss.

The Comus ball, the culmination of Mardi Gras, before the war meant the yearly gathering of society to such an extent that it was said that if the floor of the French Opera House gave way during its session there would be no more “first families” in New Orleans. Only two of the Carnival Balls, Momus and Mithras, were to be given at the opera house this year. It has not been decided where they will be held. Rex and Twelfth Night will be at the Athenaeum.

Times-Picayune, December 5, 1919, sec. 1, p. 1.

10

HISTORY OF THE URSULINES

Aged Nun's Labor of Love Preserved for Posterity

Book of Hundred and Fifty Pages in Beautiful Script Written and Illustrated by Mother Mary Theresa Who Tells Story of Ursulines of New Orleans from Their Coming Two Hundred Years Ago to Present. Chapters from Past.

This is the story of a book, and it is the story of a woman's life as well: for the two are so interlaced that one cannot separate them.

The book is large, bound in dark red leather; the lettering is in gold. It is a pleasing volume, even before you open the pages.

The woman is an Ursuline nun. The book is her life work.

Not all of her life work, of course—not even a fraction of it, for her long life has been spent in teaching young girls. But she found time to write this volume, and it stands a monument to her industry and her scholarship.

And it is a most unusual book for it is all hers. Not only did she write it, but she put it in its present form. It is not a printed volume, but is written out in beautiful French script, very large, very clear, for one hundred and fifty pages. It is illustrated with pencil and with ink drawings. You turn page after page in wonder; the writing never varies. It is always large, firm, beautifully executed. The paragraphs are headed with large illumined letters. The chapter heads are done with infinite pains, perfect to the smallest detail. Holding the volume in your hands you are reminded of the old manuscripts made by monks in the middle ages—those marvelous documents sometimes seen in museums.

The name? "Louisiana's First Educational Institution. The Ursuline Convent, New Orleans, from 1727 to the Present Day."

The title page itself is a thing to make you pause, so complicated is the design, so careful is the workmanship. There are countless scrolls, leaves and latticed designs which surround the title—perfect, perfect to the last faintly marked pen stroke.

But so much for externals! The book is there, a history of the Ursulines in Louisiana, a document for all time to come.

Before going into the matter contained in this volume, it may be well to speak of the author—Mother Mary Theresa, a venerable nun who recently celebrated her golden jubilee.

Her family name is Wolfe, and she was born seventy-four years ago in Listowell, Kerry county, Ireland. She was one of a family of thirteen children, seven of whom entered religious orders. Her oldest sister entered the Order of Presentation in her native town, as Sister Aloysius. Four brothers became Jesuits, one of whom the Reverend Patrick Wolfe, S.J., still survives. For several years he was the rector of St. Mary's college in Chesterfield, England. After completing his term of superior, he was sent as minister to St. Adon's college. During the world war he went into service as an army chaplain in England, and when the war was over and his services no longer needed he returned to scholastic life. Her brother, Richard Wolfe, is established in Australia. One of her sisters married Lawrence Ginnell, member of the British Parliament, and at present is a delegate of the Irish Republic to South America.

Mother Theresa entered the Ursuline Novitiate in Beaujeu, in the South of France, February 2, 1870 – the year of the Franco-Prussian war. She came to New Orleans at the close of the same year and received the holy habit, May 11, 1871. She made her profession May 14, 1872, in the old Ursuline convent in Dauphine street. The superiors at that time were Mother Saint Scraphine Ray, of France, and Mother Saint Augustin O'Keefe, who was in the Ursuline convent of Boston when it was set on fire. These superiors recognized Sister Theresa's abilities, who helped to establish the day school at the corner of Esplanade avenue and Rampart street in New Orleans.

In her half century of service Mother Theresa taught in the Dauphine street convent, in the Esplanade day school and in St. Angela's school. Her work has been far reaching, and she is known throughout the city in homes of former pupils. Through the years she made many friends. Girls who had loved her in the convent, married and brought up their daughters to love her. She even taught some of the grandchildren of her former pupils.

May 14, of this year, Mother Mary Theresa celebrated her golden jubilee. It was a great day in the Ursuline convent. From all quarters of the city the friends of this venerable nun came, in scores, in hundreds. The chapel and the convent halls were crowded, for Mother St. Albert, the superior, had thrown open the doors to all who knew and loved Mother Theresa. There were white haired grandmothers, their daughters, their granddaughters. How they laughed, as they talked of the old days when they were pupils of Mother Theresa—how they recalled this or that incident of bygone years.

Very Rev. Cannon Racine, rector of the convent, officiated, and Rev. Rev. Father Weldon, vicar of the archdiocese, and Rev. Michael Kenny, S.J., assisted him. Father Kenny delivered the sermon.

After the ceremony there was an informal reception in the convent. Mother Theresa received many gifts from her former pupils, and a sum of money was given to distribute as she saw fit to various charities.

It was only in discussing the Golden Jubilee with Mother Mary Theresa that the story of the history of the Ursulines came to light—

for the nun takes no credit for this monumental work—it is done for the order she says—no credit is hers.

This is very characteristic of the Ursulines—there is nothing personal in the work they accomplish, self is submerged in the whole; they work for a common end.

"But when did you ever find time to do all of this?" you ask, as you sit holding the volume on your knees, slowly turning the pages. "Why, it seems there is the work of a lifetime here!"

Mother Theresa smiles as she replies: "Oh, just at odd times—now and then. It took some time."

You wonder at her moderation. Some time! You should think so. And then you open to chapter one:

There is a picture facing the first chapter, a plan of New Orleans in 1719—just a year or so after the founding of the city in the wilderness. There are exactly eight buildings in the town, and they stand in a semi-circle of cleared land along the river. Nearest the woods is the store-house, a roughly constructed building with one large door and two windows; five cabins for workmen are scattered around the central square—which is now the Place D'Armes. The barracks are shown at the river's side, near what must be St. Peter Street today, and another large warehouse stands at what must be the lower Pontalba building in St. Ann Street.

As you look you wonder. Where, how, did this old plan come to the Ursulines? For here it is, carefully drawn, carefully numbered. This, as you know, was before the arrival of the first Ursulines.

Chapter one is devoted to the story of "The Preparation" and describes the orders which led to the founding of the convent on the Mississippi when Louisiana was young. In this chapter there is another illustration: it is "La Gironde," the sailing vessel which brought over the first Ursulines – a three-master, looking sadly inadequate for the long voyage. There is also a picture of Bienville's house, which stood somewhere near the site of the present customhouse.

> It was a two-story frame building, each floor having six apartments. The windows were numerous, but instead of being glazed each was

> furnished with a frame covered with thin linen, which while admitting the air, was almost as translucent as glass.

The picture shows the house somewhat like those still standing in the French Quarter—a long, wide structure, with six doors on the ground floor, each closed with heavy batten blinds. Above are the six windows already described. The roof is of large tiles. There are three dormer windows shown and two chimneys. The house is shown set in a garden, bounded by a high fence.

On page 27, something is told of the Natchez massacre:

> On the 13th of March, 1729, took place the imposing ceremony of Sister St. Stanislaus Hachard's profession, the first of that kind within the limits of the United States. Toward the close of the same year occurred the horrible massacre of the French at Fort Rosalle, by the Natchez Indians, whose savage nature had not yet undergone the salutary influence of the Jesuit missionaries. It may not be out of place to insert here a few passages translated from a letter written by the Rev. Father LePetit, S.J., to the Rev. Father d'Avangour, of the same society:
>
> 'My Reverend Father: You cannot be ignorant of the sad event which has destroyed part of the French colony established at Natchez, on the right bank of the Mississippi at a distance of 120 leagues from its mouth. Two of our missioners who were engaged in the conversion of the savages have been included in the almost general massacre which this barbarous nation made on the French, at a time also when they had not the least reason to suspect their perfidy. A loss so great as this infant mission has sustained will continue for a long time to excite our deepest regrets.'

What repression!

The Natchez massacre was one of the most dreadful things of early Louisiana history. Can one, in this day and age, imagine writing so calmly of a great disaster which left but a few survivors?

There is something of this great repression felt throughout the pages of Mother Theresa's volume. She tells incidents, gives names and dates in the most concise way – only at times does she lapse into personalities, and that is when she quotes from letters and old documents. And how interesting they are!

In recounting the story of the first convent and military hospital —the building still stands at Ursuline and Chartres streets—Mother Theresa says:

> On the evening of July 17, 1734, the Ursulines removed to the monastery, for which, we are told, they sighed as ardently as had, of yore, the Israelites for the Promised Land. The removal has been thus described by a member of the community:
>
> 'During the three days previous to the one appointed for our removal to the new convent, it rained almost incessantly, making the roads so impassible that we were on the point of giving up the idea of leaving our residence so soon, when suddenly the sky cleared up; and, in spite of the muddy roads, we decided on taking possession of our new home ere the setting of the sun.
>
> 'Accordingly, toward five o'clock in the afternoon, our convent bells rang a merry peal to announce our decision. Immediately the troops arranged themselves on both sides of the abode which we were about to leave forever. Governor Bienville, Mr. Salmon, intendant, together with the most distinguished citizens and almost the entire population, came to form our escort.
>
> 'After the benediction of the Blessed Sacrament, which was given by the Rev. Father Philips, Franciscan, assisted by the Rev. Fathers de Beaubois and Le Petit, all left the chapel in processional order; the citizens opening the march, followed by the orphans, day scholars, and about forty of the most respectable ladies of the town, all bearing lighted tapers and singing pious hymns. Next came about twenty young girls dressed in white, who were followed by twelve others, representing St. Ursula and her companions, and several little girls dressed as angels.
>
> 'The young girl who impersonated St. Ursula wore a costly robe and mantle, and a crown glittering with diamonds and pearls, from

which hung a rich veil of graceful folds; in her hand she bore a heart pierced with an arrow. Her companions were clad in snow white dresses and veils; and they bore palm branches, emblematic of the great and glorious victory won by the heroic band of virgin martyrs whom they had the honor of representing.

'Last of all came the religious and the clergy; the former bearing lighted tapers, and the latter a rich canopy under which the Blessed Sacrament was carried in triumph. The soldiers marched on each side, leaving a space of about four feet between them and the procession. The military march which accompanied the singing of pious hymns, contributed not a little to the beauty and impressiveness of the ceremony.

'As soon as the procession was within sight of the convent, some kind friend commenced to ring the bells, in order to hail our arrival; thus we entered our new abode, to the chiming of bells, fifes and drums, the singing of hymns and praise and thanksgiving to our Heavenly Father whose providence had lavished on us so many favors.

'On entering the chapel, places were assigned to us in the sanctuary, where we remained during the sermon and benediction which followed. The blessed Sacrament having been placed on the altar and incensed, the soldiers sang a hymn in honor of the Holy Eucharist, and another in honor of our glorious patron St. Ursula; after which Father Le Petit, S.J., delivered a very touching and eloquent discourse in which he set forth the necessity and advantage of giving youth a solid Christian education. The Reverend Father spoke also, in glowing words, of how much our labors had contributed to promote the glory of God and the welfare of the colony.

'After the benediction of the Blessed Sacrament, the people retired, apparently edified and pleased; and we were delighted to find ourselves once more secluded from the world.'

How real it all seems—even after 200 years! And how vividly this Ursuline makes the picture seem. Written, as it is, in Mother Theresa's fine flowing script, it has something of the character of the original document, painstaking, truthfully vivid.

The whole history of the Ursulines in Louisiana lies spread before you. Reading through the pages you are able to follow them, step by step through the years—their leave taking of the old convent, and their welcome to the new.

You reach the last page and pause for a moment it seems, almost, that a light shines from the pages, that the faith which inspired this work is making itself manifest. No thought of self: all is for the good of the order and the glory of God—Yes, it is plain enough.

There is a moment of silence as you close the book.

Times-Picayune Magazine Section, June 4, 1922, p. 3.

11

FRENCH TOWN CHANGES WITH COMING OF AUTO

Paving Takes the Place of Cobblestones—Old Inhabitants Are Brought Face to Face With Modern Times.

"Mon ami!" cries Delphine, a little dressmaker of Royal street as she peers out between the green shutters, "Look, ma mere! A pink automobile is coming out of de courtyard across the street! I cannot believe my eyes, but I assure you it is the truth!"

The last few years have brought a great change to Royal street. As Delphine contemplated the "pink" automobile outside of her little shop, her mind ran back to other days when Royal street was a cobbled roadway with grass growing between the cobble stones.

It has not been long—only four years—since Royal street from Toulouse street to Esplanade, and beyond, was all cobbles and holes; traffic was practically impossible. The few old families who are left in the section of Royal street north of Toulouse, and who still retained the family carriage, were almost unable to keep their seats in these antique coaches, so rough was the road.

It was amusing to watch them, the little faded old ladies, driving out in the late afternoons of summer, with little black carriage-parasols tilted against the sun, and their trim bonnets and thread mits. How dainty they looked, and how badly shaken up they were, as the horse dragged the carriage with difficulty over the rough street.

It's all changed now. And it has been the result of the automobile. Royal street, nowadays, presents a flat, even surface surpassing most of the uptown thoroughfares, and all day long—and all night, the constant hum of automobiles are heard, as the cars race "uptown" toward Canal street.

Nor is Royal street alone in this. Several cross streets, Toulouse, and others near Canal, are paved, and at present the work of paving St. Peter and St. Ann streets goes apace. When these streets are finished, as they will be soon, there will be a good road-way in front of both of the Pontalba buildings, and Jackson Square will be connected with Royal street with several paved streets.

And it is well that this is so, for, since the opening of the Quartier Club in the house of the Daughters of 1812, adjoining the Cabildo, there has been a constant group of motor cars lined up near the Cathedral. "Society" has found the French Quarter again after a lapse of many years.

The situation, according to little Delphine the dressmaker, is akin to the chicken and the egg. "Me, I cannot tell," says she. "Did the paved streets bring the automobiles, or did the automobiles pave the streets—just like the chicken and the egg: Me, I can never tell which of them God made first: I'd like to know!"

Delphine is a simple soul, but she knows, for all that. And also, she is determined to find out about the "pink" automobile.

All day long she thinks about that strange and beautiful motor car that drove out of the courtyard across the way, and in her mind, she pictures romances: "Who owns the car? What is it doing in the Delange courtyard? Perhaps Lola Delange has a rich suitor? Who knows?"

Late in the afternoon Miss Delange came into Delphine's shop to ask for a dress that Delphine was repairing for her, and then the story came out. The Delanges have sold their carriage and horses and have bought an automobile.

"For me, for Christmas," says Miss Delange, in answer to Delphine's question, "Everyone has a car nowadays, and horses, except to ride, are passé," she assures Delphine.

And Delphine told everyone who came into her shop about the new automobile. It has set her to thinking:

"Ma mère," she said to her mother at bed-time, as the two of them sat drinking hot milk in the tiny kitchen back of the shop, "how would you like to have an automobile?"

"My child, you are mad, I assure you," remarked her mother unperturbed.

"But no," said Delphine, "me, I have saved up nearly six hundred dollars, and for that amount, ma mère, we could buy a little second hand—how you say?—a second hand flivver. It would be a benefit to one's health, and me! Would I learn to make her go? Oui! Oui!"

"Mais non!" said her mother, "you'll kill yourself, you! You great goose!"

But Delphine is thinking all the same. And a "second hand flivver" holds all her attention now. All day long, as she sits at her sewing, she is thinking of it. A car all her own! Has she not as much room in her courtyard as the Delanges? She could take care of it herself!

So do not be surprised if, some afternoon, you meet Delphine in a flivver. It will probably be out near City Park, for Delphine prefers the "downtown" New Orleans to the "uptown" districts – and it is natural enough for she was born, brought up, and shall probably die in the old house in Royal street.

"But, if I can get that flivver, I shall die content!" says she, as her needle goes rapidly to and fro in the waning light.

Times-Picayune, December 19, 1920, sec. 5, p. 1.

12

GLORIES OF THE PAST RECALLED BY PASSING OF PONTALBA BUILDING

Another of Landmarks of Old City on Market

Heirs in France Want Division of Estate, So Upper Pontalba Buildings Are to Be Offered for Sale—Closely Connected With Glories of Old City.

Another of the landmarks of the old New Orleans is to be sold, the Pontalba building, facing Jackson Square, has been offered for sale by the heirs of the Baroness Pontalba—that picturesque figure of the old city when it stood in its greater glory.

One of the buildings has been sold already. A group of men—who choose to remain anonymous—bought the northern row of these old red brick buildings early in the year. Now news comes from Paris that the heirs of the baroness are asking for a division of property, and the southern row, those looking north across Jackson Square, are to be offered for sale for $66,000.

The sale of these buildings may mean the ruin of the French Quarter, or it may mean that a decided step will be taken to preserve the historic square from destruction. Jackson square is perhaps the one part of the Vieux Carré which is practically as it was in the old days when society lived in the shadow of the Cathedral. Facing the square there are only the two Pontalba buildings, the Cathedral, the Cabildo and the Presbytère. The fourth side of the square—that which faced the river formerly, has been raised by the erection of freight sheds and docks, but the square itself is practically unchanged. It is still beautiful, still tranquil, still dignified and still the center of the old city.

Illustration 3. *The Lower Pontalba Building. Detroit Publishing Company, ca. 1910. Retrieved from the Library of Congress.*

History of the Building

Much has been written about the Pontalba buildings, but then, conversely, much has happened there, not historic things perhaps apart from the visit of Lafayette, but all the little intimate things that make the social life of old New Orleans so fascinating to read about, to hear about, and to think about.

It was in 1819 that the Baroness Pontalba, the beautiful Michaela, daughter of Don Almonaster Pontalba Y Rojas, built these two rows of houses because, it is said, "she didn't like the gloomy houses of Royal street"—and that these houses were to combine something of both the Spanish and French styles of architecture—in other words, to express something of the personality of Michaela herself.

So they were built, long rows of houses, with something peculiarly attractive about them—a sort of charm that is only felt in houses that have been built for homes. Each building contained twelve houses, and twelve stores below—for the Baroness, for all her artistic temperament, was a business woman as well.

Old people of the city tell wonderful tales of the extravagancies of the baroness. The stores rented each for $1000 a month. The baroness lived in the central house in the northern row of buildings—her windows looked out over the square and the warm Southern breeze blew in her front windows. The rooms in this particular house are tremendous. Even in their dilapidation today there is seen something of the dignity and grandeur of the salon of madame.

Crystal chandeliers flooded the drawing rooms with light, marble mantels covered with delicate tracery added charm to the rooms. One hears strange stories of the luxurious tastes of madame; that her liveried servants stood outside at all hours of the day and night to open the carriage door of those who went to call.

Social Life in the Fifties

Madame's neighbors were the most fashionable in the city. There were other titles besides hers bound behind the red brick façade of the houses. Social life in the fifties was particularly gay. Balls and receptions were nightly events. There was opera, too, nearby. All night long, the old people tell us, volumes of late revelers sounded through the Place D'Armes—and duels and "coffee for two" were the fashion of the near vicinity—the coffee in the French Market around the corner, and the duels in what is now City Park, or if the blood of the duelists was too hot to wait, duels were fought in St. Anthony's Garden, directly behind the Cathedral.

There was scandal in those days, too—as there is scandal in these. On Orleans street, just around the corner, there stood the old Orleans Theater. Here the quadroon balls were held. It is said that many tears were shed by the society girls in those days, because the handsome sweethearts and brothers deserted the fashionable ballrooms to "look in" at the quadroon balls in the Orleans Theater ballroom. And it was the sub-rosa life that led to the duels in the early morning, the old people say.

At any event, the Pontalba buildings were the center of the Creole life of that period—the splendid fifties—for ten years after the Civil war brought novelty to New Orleans, and social life declined, not to resume its luxury and its magnificence even to this day—that is, of course, if you can believe the stories of those who lived then, and who saw with their own eyes. Things, of course, have a way of getting brighter, the farther off they are; perhaps the magnificence was not really so magnificent—who knows? But at any rate, the Pontalba buildings saw it all—all the grandeur, all the romance, all the heart-burnings of the social life of the old New Orleans.

Evil Days Fall

Later—much later—evil days fell to the old buildings. The baroness Pontalba returned to Paris, and died there. The heirs remained abroad. The buildings here were handled by agents. The tenants left and the buildings remained practically vacant for years.

Then came the days of the tenements. The buildings were rented for as low as $16 per month to the foreign born.[29] Troops of noisy children invaded the old courtyards; wreckage piled up in the halls. The crystal chandeliers were taken away, the marble mantels were dragged from their palaces. The worst possible treatment was given the old houses.

But in Michaela Pontalba's day, they built houses—not the flimsy little structures that we build today. The houses stood there, even in their decay and dilapidation, possessing a certain dignity that even row upon row of clothes drying in the sun could not take away.

The buildings still are tenements. Of course, there is the exception. Le Petit Theater Du Vieux Carré leased the river corner of the northern row of buildings, and opened its little playhouse there. Society returned once more to the Pontalba buildings. But there was a difference. Now it is an odd thing to do—to go and spend the evening in Jackson Square. Once, it was the natural thing to do—once it was the thing most envied—an invitation to spend an evening in the Pontalba buildings—it raised one's reputation socially. Other times, other manners, as the old people say when they talk of it.

But what will become of the Pontalba buildings now? Who will buy them? What will be their future? If one only knew! Or perhaps it is best that we cannot know—those of us who love the old New Orleans.

Buying the Past

But there is this to be said. Whoever buys the Pontalba buildings buys much more than the mere shell of a house. For there is the past to contend with. Say what you wish—call it imagination, superstition, what you will—but there hangs over the old buildings a feeling that time cannot change. There is the feeling that the buildings know their glorious past. There is the self-possession they possess that even the tenement dwellers cannot change.

Pause for a moment in one of the vast empty rooms. Keep still—from somewhere out of the past there will come a whisper. If you are a sensitive person—if you are susceptible to these things—you can hear it plainly not the words perhaps, but the sound of them: "Look!" the whisper seems to say, "Look! I am the Baroness Pontalba! I built these houses for my whim! These houses belong to me! Nobody can take them away from me. My personality is still here. I am still here!"

If whispers from the past do not interest you—there are other things. Lafayette was entertained in these buildings; Jenny Lind lived there; Adelina Patti visited them; Sarah Bernhardt has visited friends living there.[30] The old buildings are rich in memories, as they are rich in whispers. The man who buys the Pontalba buildings will not buy a house; he will buy countless memories, countless recollections—memories which lurk in the shadow of the old stairs, memories which are tangled in the cobweb of the old walls.

Memories and cobweb—history and whispers. He who buys the Pontalba buildings will buy all these, to keep, to hold, and in time, to learn to love.

For there is no place in America that possesses such a vast wealth of untold stories—stories that will, perhaps, never be told except to those who live in the old buildings and who may dream the stories as they sit in the old candle-lit rooms, drowsing by the fire on long winter evenings.

Times-Picayune, November 7, 1920, sec. 3, p. 1.

13

CHARM OF THE OLD FRENCH QUARTER QUICKLY SETTLES UPON ITS VISITORS

WHAT VISITORS CAN SEE IN FAMOUS VIEUX CARRÉ

How Tour on Foot Can Be Made from the Courthouse to Esplanade Avenue, and Description of Places of Greatest Historical Interest in New Orleans

Would you like to visit Frenchtown unchaperoned by the usual guide? Do you care to wander at will along the quaint old streets of the Vieux Carré? If you do, friend tourist, get your hat and come along with me. We'll start in the late afternoon, because at that time the soft colors of evening will fall across the battered façades of the old houses and will treat them kindly. They are like wrinkled faces, these old houses, and one must look upon them with the deference that youth should show to age. The houses have outlived their usefulness, like so many of the old, and while you may look as much as you please, you must look with friendly eyes. If you do not, you may come away with only the ideas of dirt and squalor—

and you may miss altogether the lingering charm, which clings to the old mansions, even in the last stages of their decay.

How shall we make the trip? Walk, of course. The Quarter is small, only about ten squares from end to end, and less than that distance from the river to Rampart street. Why do they call it the Vieux Carré? It means, literally, "old square," that's all, the old square, which made the walled city of Nouvelle Orleans, when Americans, as you and I, did not profane the streets. Are you ready? Very well, we'll start at once.

We'll leave Canal street at Royal, and turn from our present-day world. Yes, Royal street is the same as St. Charles, but the name changes when Canal street is crossed. Notice how narrow the streets are, and notice how the balconies overhang the sidewalks. By the way, friend tourist, we call the sidewalks "banquettes"—that's a Creole word—no, not French, just plain Creole. No, you won't find it in the French dictionary.[31] It's a word that's particularly our own.

Modern needs are pushing the Quarter farther and farther from Canal street. We'll walk hastily along the street until we are past the Monteleone Hotel—Oh, wait—Don't forget to look at the old Union Bank at Iberville and Royal streets. That is one of the oldest bank buildings here. See, the structure is almost covered with that new addition that forms shops in front. Look up. That's right; notice the old columns. Looks colonial, doesn't it? Stop, if you will, and gaze into the windows of the antique shops. There are many beautiful things to be found here. Antique shops are the most interesting, and the most tragic things imaginable. How tragic? Well, they contain the wreckage of old families, mostly Creole families—people who once had everything their hearts desired. Where are they now, Lord, I don't know. Here are their most cherished possessions. Can't you be satisfied with that?

What does "Creole" mean? No, of course not. I don't know why tourists always say that. The Creole is not of colored blood. The word means of French or Spanish descent, or of mixed descent, French and Spanish. The Creole is one who is born away from his country—whatever that country may be. The New Orleans Creole is our finest product. The women are lovely. The men are brave. They have charming manners. They are exclusive. They are clannish. Can anyone blame them? They have their own language, their own society, their own customs. What language did they speak? They still speak a pure French. The reason the word "Creole" has been so often misunderstood is because their slaves spoke a Creole dialect, bearing about the same relation to pure French as our Southern negro talk does to English purely spoken. Then, of course, there was the Acadian French, or "Cajun" French, as spoken in the outlying districts of Louisiana. And "Gumbo" French—that means simply French incorrectly spoken.

Illustration 4. *The Paul Morphy House on Royal street. Drawing by Frank G. Churchill. Taken from: Lyle Saxon, "Charm of the Old French Quarter Quickly Settles on Its Visitors," the* Times-Picayune, *February 15, 1920, sec. 3, p. 1.*

Here we are at Royal and Conti streets, three squares from Canal. Let us stop here, in front of the courthouse. I'll point out the interesting houses from here.

The courthouse is new, of course. It was built in 1910. But at the corner, the southeast corner, is the old Hall of Mortgages. It is the Bank of Louisiana, built in 1812. Notice how interesting it is architecturally. Do you see its irregularity? The pilasters are not the same distance apart. The pedestals on the cornice are not placed above the pilasters. And even the urns on the pedestals are not placed in the center of the pedestals. Irregular? Of course, but following the law of symmetry, nevertheless. That's what gives these old houses their intense personality. Do you see what I mean? Look closely.

Notice the iron scrollwork on the balconies of that antique shop on the opposite corner—the southwest corner. All hand-hammered, wrought-iron. It is very beautiful. They tell us that it was all made in workshops here, hammered out by negro slaves. It is priceless today, and it cannot be duplicated.

Notice the huge old mansion opposite on the northwest corner. The shop below is called "The Antique Dome" on account of the vaulted ceiling inside. This was another bank building. Notice the monogram in the ironwork upon the balcony. The building is particularly typical of the residences of its day. Did "first families" live above shops? You bet they did. Some of them still do. Those rooms have most magnificent old marble mantelpieces and crystal chandeliers.

Now turn your attention to the old Paul Morphy house at 417 Royal street. Notice the round windows on the third floor. The Creole was fond of window decoration. This building was also a bank once. The banker's family lived above. Later the Morphy family lived there. Paul Morphy was the world's greatest chess player. They tell us he used to play in the courtyard. Yes, you can go in. The court is one of the loveliest in the city. Do you see the magnolia trees growing here? In the spring they are filled with tremendous flowers. One can lean on the balcony and pick them. Yes, this is a lovely place, but we can't stay here all day. There are lovelier things to come. We'll continue down Royal Street.

At the corner of Royal and St. Louis, where the signboards disfigure the street, there stood the old St. Louis Hotel. In its day it was the most fashionable hotel in the South. It was torn down in 1917.

Yes, a great pity. It should have been preserved. From this corner look toward the river there at Chartres and St. Louis, stands the Napoleon House. It has a red cupola; you can't miss it. They tell us this house was actually built for Napoleon. Built and furnished for him. Think what it might have meant to New Orleans if Napoleon had been rescued from St. Helena! It was a plot fostered by the young Creole bloods of the old New Orleans. The plan was to send a light sailing vessel for him, as he languished on St. Helena. Dominique You, one of Lafitte the Pirate's lieutenants, was to head the expedition. On the eve of sailing the news reached New Orleans that Napoleon was dead. Governor Girod afterward occupied the house. It was recently sold for $14,000. It's an old Italian tenement now. It's an interesting old place, don't you think? The architecture is very fine. Notice the ironwork. It's good. All right? Let's continue down Royal street.

In the Old Section

Just next door to the site of the St. Louis Hotel, there is an interesting place. The courtyard gate is open. Go in and look around. Do you see that the windows which face the courtyard are fan-shaped, Spanish influence. Notice the open balcony on the roof in the rear. Notice the large slave quarters. They have been converted into a storage warehouse now, but never mind—you can see what they were once.

Now we really have reached the old section of the city. Note the overhanging balconies the individual balconies for the third-story windows. Can't you imagine the Creole beauties, leaning out, looking down, waving a scarf to her suitor, perhaps? Notice the old house on the southwest corner of Royal and Toulouse streets. It has the Egyptian design on the pilasters supporting the roof. That was the influence of Napoleon's visit to Egypt. Egyptian fashions were popular in all Europe then. It seems odd, doesn't it, that because he went to Egypt there should be Egyptian designs in the French Quarter of New Orleans? That is the reason, nevertheless. The entrance to this old house is in Toulouse street. Notice the lions on the gateway. Look above the gate and see the palms growing in the courtyard beyond.

Illustration 5. *View through Orleans street of rear of St. Louis Cathedral. Drawing by Frank G. Churchill. Taken from: Lyle Saxon, "Charm of the Old Frrench Quarter Quickly Settles on Its Visitors,"* Times-Picayune, *February 15, 1920, sec. 3, p. 1.*

But to continue down Royal street. Go into the courtyard at 618 Royal by all means. Yes, this is the one you see on postcards; it is typical. Notice the old iron fountain, notice the formal flower beds. Go to the back and look at the house. Note its beautiful irregularity. Don't take any photographs, however. The owners do not like it, and you must remember that the courtyards are private property. Go in when you see a gate open, but remember that the owner is doing you a favor. Tourists forget this sometimes, and for this reason some courtyards are kept closed. Nearly every heavy-barred double gate you see hides some courtyard from your vision. If any are open in this neighborhood peep in. You will be surprised at what you see. There are palms, palmettos, statues and even fountains. The Creoles who built those houses a hundred or more years ago like to have their coffee and company in the court.

Some of the old families still live in this block—the 600 block—and on warm evenings you can see them on the balconies, old ladies mostly, old like their houses, but with the same lingering charm.

The house at 637 Royal street, a house of two stories with arched windows, was the residence of Adelina Patti, the great singer, when she made her home in New Orleans. Look into the court, if the door is open; there is a garden behind the house.

Center of Old Social Life

At the end of the next block, you will find a small square just back of the cathedral. This is St. Anthony's garden, where duels were fought in the old days. Orleans street ends here. Standing at Royal and Orleans streets, you can see the old Orleans Theater, the scene of the notorious quadroon balls. It is a convent of colored sisters now. The Convent of the Holy Family. Go in, if you have a chance. The colored nuns will show you through, if they are not busy, and if you will, leave a little offering for the negro children, the little orphans which the good sisters are caring for.

Be sure and notice the old houses which flank St. Anthony's Garden. They are most interesting, and are among the oldest standing in the Quarter. Walk through the alley—either one—toward the river, and you will emerge at Jackson Square, the old Place

D'Armes. This was the very enter of social life in the old New Orleans. From the center of the Square, you can see the Cabildo, the Cathedral, the Presbytery, and the Pontalba Buildings. The Cabildo now is the State Museum, and is open to the public. If you are interested in the old New Orleans, take an hour and wander through. There are enough relics there to enable you to construct the whole life of the Creoles. The paintings of the types existing in war times and before are particularly interesting. Notice the beauty of the women—notice the poetic expression of the young men. You don't see faces like these nowadays. Our commercial spirit has killed the poetry in young men's faces. In the museum is the Death Mask of Napoleon.

The Cabildo was erected in 1795 and was the scene of the transfer of Louisiana from France to the United States in 1803. Later it was the city hall, and still later it housed Lafayette when he visited New Orleans in 1826.

The St. Louis Cathedral stands where the first church of New Orleans stood, in 1720. The present building was erected by Don Almonaster Y. Roxas, and presented to his fellow Catholics in 1794.

The building flanking the Cathedral on the other side is the "Presbytere" built in 1813. Formerly it was the Civil District Court. Now it is a museum.

Now, just a word about the square itself. It was laid out by Bienville, founder of New Orleans, in 1718. The American Flag was unfurled there in 1803, to mark the possession of the United States, after the transfer of Louisiana from France. A statue of General Jackson, designed by Clark Mills, marks the spot where the flag was raised.

The Pontalba Buildings

Before you leave the square, you must look well at the Pontalba Buildings which form the northern and southern boundary. They were built by Michaela, the daughter of Don Almonaster Pontalba. You can see the Pontalba monogram in hundreds of places, woven in the iron work. At one time these houses were filled with the most aristocratic families of the old city. Jenny Lind, Adelina Patti, Lafayette, and countless other celebrities visited the families living there.

Illustration 6. *The Haunted House, Royal and Hospital streets. Drawing by Frank G. Churchill. Taken from: Lyle Saxon, "Charm of the Old French Quarter Quickly Settles on Its Visitors,"* Times-Picayune, *February 15, 1920, sec. 3, p. 1.*

There are many other places of interest, friend tourist, and I'd like to wander further with you, but the shadow of the cathedral has crossed the square and has reached the river. Darkness is falling over the old houses, covering them with her friendly dusk, covering the battered facades with a kindly veil. Wander further, if you like, there is still the French Market, the Old Archbishop's Palace, the Beauregard home, the haunted house, and countless other fascinating places. But you must go alone. There are guide-books which will tell you about the places to see. There are guides which may be engaged by the hour. But, in all of your wanderings, remember this:

The old New Orleans was a city of intense personality. Time and decay has not killed this pristine charm. The old houses today are as full of beauty as they were in their prime. Architecturally, they are vastly interesting. Stay for a while in the old section of the city. Sit for a while in Jackson Square; let the old world soak in. Give the atmosphere a chance to reach you. Take your time and wander slowly. Look twice at the old houses. They are worth it. Talk to the beggars, talk to anyone you chance to meet. The natives of the Quarter are a kindly folk, and they will gladly tell you anything they happen to know. Those who live in the quarter live there because they like it; they are proud of the old houses. They like your admiration, and your interest. Go where you will, do what you please, you will not be molested, nor will you be annoyed. Take your time and wander through, and then, friend tourist, if you have a heart in you, you will want to return. For in the Vieux Carré of New Orleans, and in the Vieux Carré alone, you will find that lingering charm of the old world, that remnant of a bygone culture which is unique in America.

Times-Picayune, February 15, 1920, sec. 3, p. 1.

14

POTTERY SPECIMENS INTRIGUE ADMIRERS OF THE CERAMIC ART AT BILOXI

WONDERFUL CRAFTSMANSHIP SHOWN BY BILOXI POTTER

Productions of Rare Loveliness Exhibited Alongside Grotesque, Distorted and Futurist Types, All Displaying Unusual Genius of Their Maker.

Within a scant half-square of a busy street in Biloxi, Miss., there stands a small, shuttered cottage. It seems half forgotten there, left behind by the seasons which have passed over its long-gabled roof; summer suns and storms of winter have left their marks upon it; and the rains of years have mellowed the cottage to a soft, undefinable color rather more gray than brown, but neither one nor the other.

A narrow flight of stairs leads down from the closed door to the sidewalk, and the shutters of the window next to the door are partly ajar. Within are seen shelves filled with rows of pottery, dull and lustrous; some of the pieces are almost classic in their chaste simplicity, while others are grotesque and distorted, willfully misshapen.

Below the shelves in a corner of the window frame is a small discolored sign: "Pottery for sale."

You pause and stand looking at the vessels displayed there; you walk closer and examine them, arrested by their beauty, intrigued by their strangeness. For never have you seen craftsmanship which bore the mark of the maker to such a degree. What is the potter like—this man who has made these strange and fanciful designs?

You knock, but there is no reply, no sound except the steady hammering of iron on steel in a blacksmith shop nearby. The steady heat of noon falls around you; the hum of insects fills the air. Slowly, as in a dream, you turn the knob and cross the threshold.

You find yourself in a room which is filled from end to end with pottery; it stands upon shelves, upon the floor, in the window sills; tables are covered with it, and, as you look through the door of the adjoining room, you see other pieces of pitchers, cups of luster ware, vases, jars, lamps jumbled together in confusion—a veritable museum of spheres, globes and rhomboids as well as pieces of irregular shapes which you cannot name.

Standing there in the stillness, surrounded by these strange vessels, you find yourself speaking aloud—a half-forgotten verse of Omar Khayyam:

As under cover of the departing Day
Slunk hunger-stricken Ramazan away.
Once more within the Potter's house alone
I stood, surrounded by the Shapes of Clay.

Shapes of all Sorts and Sizes, great and small,
That stood along the floor and by the wall.
And some loquacious Vessels were; and some
Listened perhaps, but never talked at all.

Said one among them—"Surely not in vain
My substance of the common Earth was ta'en
And to this Figure molded, to be broke,

Or trampled back to shapeless Earth again."

Then said a second—"Ne'er a peevish Boy
Would break the Bowl from which he drank in joy;
And He that with his hand the Vessel made
Will surely not in after Wrath destroy."

After a momentary silence spake
Some Vessel of a more ungainly Make;
"They sneer at me for leaning all awry;
What! Did the hand of the Potter shake?'

Whereat some one of the loquacious Lot—
I think a Sufi pipkin—waxing hot—
"All this of Pot and Potter—Tell me then,
Who is the Potter, pray, and who is the Pot?"

"Why," said another, "Some there are who tell
Of one who threatens he will toss to Hell
The luckless Pots he marr'd in making—Pish!
He's a good fellow, and 'twill all be well."

There is something almost uncanny in the room. As you turn from one piece of pottery to another, you are amazed to see how strongly the potter has marked these pieces of clay with his own strange personality. And what a genius for the grotesque the potter has! Yes, grotesque, that is the exact word; fantastic, too weird.

You are holding a silver lacquered teapot, a beautifully conceived and executed design, simple and lovely in line. The potter is a master —and yet, as you replace it on his shelf, you are almost shocked at the ungainliness of the piece next to it, an unwieldy jar, top-heavy, fantastically, comically ugly, with three handles, all placed awry, as if with malicious intent. A veritable monster of a pot. Perverse, but humorous too. Yes, that's it. Humorous. You can almost hear the potter's chuckle as he turned it on the potter's wheel. A slap in the face of conventional art—futuristic! The potter is a futurist; he has tired of the beautiful, and finds joy in the bizarre, the ugly.

Suddenly, you find yourself liking the potter immensely. You can imagine his personality: genial, yet canny and wise; a master of his art, yet a joker. Ah, here is a man who can laugh at life, even while life buffets him about. You must meet this man. You want to know him—or perhaps you know him already—as one knows a writer, by the things he writes. Only, in this instance, you feel that you know the potter better than you could ever know a writer—for here is bare, stark personality in every jar and jug.

A footstep is heard in the adjoining room, and you turn, almost guiltily from the shelves before you. A woman appears on the threshold. You inquire for the potter. There is something shocking in her answer:

"He died four years ago last April."

BUT YOU WERE RIGHT in judging the man's personality—that personality which has outlasted his life-time, and has been moulded into every piece of pottery that he left behind him. A long conversation with his widow brought out these facts:

George Ohr—for such was the potter's name—was an eccentric, a man of dark complexion, with dark, piercing eyes and long hair. His moustache was so long that he wound it around his ears.

He was born in Biloxi, Miss., where his father and mother had come when they left Germany some ten years prior to the Civil war. George Ohr was born July 12, 1857. His father was a blacksmith, and used to tell his son how he had shod the first horse in Biloxi. The boy attended the elementary school in his native town, but when he was 14 years old, he went to New Orleans, where he worked in a ship chandler's shop. Later he went to sea. But the sea had no charms for him, and after one voyage, he was glad to return to Biloxi and to his father. He was still in his teens when he went to work for a Mr. Myers, who had a pottery on Back Bay, and it was there that he learned his trade. Later he established a pottery of his own in Biloxi, where he made flower pots and water jars, and went from house to house, peddling them in a wheelbarrow. In his early 20's, he married Miss Josephine Gearaine, who survives him, and who is owner of the vast store of pottery. All went well for a long time, and the fame of the potter spread. He attended expositions, displaying his wares, and winning prizes. In 1894 his pottery and home were destroyed by fire. He was left penniless, but managed to raise $800 in Biloxi, with which he rebuilt his workshop. The next year he won a prize in the Atlanta Exposition, and in 1904 he won another at St. Louis. But—and here's the eccentric quality of the man—he refused to sell one piece of his pottery at the exposition, because, he said, nobody really appreciated it. They were not willing to pay enough for it. It was art, high art, he contended, almost priceless. So, at the close of the exhibition, he was penniless. Stubbornly, he refused to sell his "clay babies" as he called them, and went to work, teaching how to make pottery, until he made enough money to return home, bringing with him the great boxes of his wares.

It was after this that isolated orders began to come to George Ohr to his pottery in Biloxi—a collector in Paris sent for some pieces; one New York art store ordered some of his work. At each of the orders his spirits rose—Ah, at last, here was real appreciation. But there were few of these orders, and he refused, point-blank to sell for less than he considered the pottery's worth.

Lean years followed. Times were bad. Once in a while he sold a few pieces, but that was all. He was sensitive too. He packed a large box of fifty pieces as a present to Delgado Museum in New Orleans. Those in charge of the museum admired the work, and made a selection of twelve pieces for their permanent exhibition; there was not room for more, they explained by letter. Ohr was furious. All or nothing. "Send it all back immediately," he wrote. And accordingly, in due time, the large crate arrived. It still stands today in his bedroom in Biloxi, unopened, still as the museum returned it to him.

For twenty years he struggled, rarely making a living for his family, enduring hunger, to realize his ideals. His widow remembers the things he used to say: "Shapes come to potter as verses to the poet. Clay follows the fingers, and the fingers follow the mind."

Every day he worked. More than 10,000 pieces were in his cottage and pottery at the time of his death. They still are there.

Once, wholly disgusted with the lack of appreciation for those around him, those who could not see his pottery with an artist's eye, he decided to bury some of it for future generations. Accordingly, at night, by the light of a lantern, he walked in the woods along Back bay, and at intervals, buried his treasures. "Someday," chuckled to himself, "men will dig these up. They will be amazed." Small wonder that his reputation as an eccentric grew and grew. But he would laugh and say: "When I am gone my work will be prized, honored and cherished. It will come."

When his wife had finished telling the story of George Ohr's life, she brought out an old cardboard box full of pictures and letters. What a treasury of humor! Here was the funny side of George Ohr—Oh, how he loved to laugh and joke. Never was there a carnival or Mardi Gras that he did not masquerade. Once he dressed as Father Time, and with a long scythe he stood in the Biloxi streets, uttering prophesies. He wore a night shirt, and a long white beard. Hundreds crowded around to hear his strange predictions. They still talk of this in Biloxi.

And then, Ohr had a passion for being photographed. There were dozens of photographs of him in the most fantastic costumes and attitudes. In one he was shown yawning, tipped back in a chair, his long white mustache wound around his ears. In another, he is standing in a strong breeze, and his whiskers float in the air, fully two feet to his left. There are many so-called "trick photographs" in which Ohr appears half a dozen times in the same picture, seated at a table, offering himself a drink of beer, or in some other fantastic position. One, particularly humorous, shows him emerging from both ends of an open barrel, looking surprised and pleased to see himself at the other end!

And all of this strange personality is shown in his work—that work that he thought priceless, and which he would never sell. This life work is now stored in boxes in a garage next door to his former cottage. There are huge crates, scores of them, each filled with dozens of pieces—and each piece is different. His widow wishes to sell the lot. She feels that she must. But she wishes to sell it all together. If some large concern would buy the lot, she would sell for $1 each. Some of the pieces—many of them—are valued at from $10 to $50 each. The smallest of them sell for more than $1.

But here a difficulty presents itself. What concern, either in New Orleans or New York, is large enough to buy 10,000 pieces of pottery at one fell swoop? And yet, could a purchaser be found, it is certain that he could make money in this way. For Ohr's pottery is rarely beautiful. He managed to make a luster ware that is superb—it rivals the old luster which is sought so eagerly in antique shops. There are hundreds of luster pieces: cups, mugs, vases, teapots without end.

What will be the fate of this collection? Will it be scattered, sold for a song? Will it disappear from the earth? And will our grandchildren, or our great, grandchildren, years from now, search the antique shops in quest of an old cracked mug, offering fabulous prices for a piece of pottery signed by George Ohr?

Let us call it tomorrow's tangle. For these questions can only be answered by time. Or to quote Omar Khayyam again:

The Moving Finger writes; and having writ;
Moves on: nor all your Piety nor Wit
Shall lure it back to cancel half a Line,
Nor all your Tears wash out a Word of it.

Times-Picayune Magazine Section, October 1, 1922, p. 5.

CHARACTER SKETCHES

15

THE ACTRESS

Hates Life of Actress

Choosing a Vocation

Stage Life Stupid, Says Fritzi Scheff, and Lure of Applause Not Fit Reward for Hard Work and Inconvenience of Traveling—Has No Love for Profession Which Brings Her Success

The curtain had just fallen and the descending wall of canvas cut off the audience from the stage. From beyond that wall there came a muffled sound of applause above the blare of the orchestra. And Fritzi Scheff, catching up her scarlet fish-tail train over one arm, came running to the wings.

"Aha!" she cried, "you think this is fun? It's work—that's what this is, work!"

She is the same old Fritzi of other years; still full of the joy of life, still talking with her quick impetuous sentences. As she strode toward her dressing room the heavy beads rattled around her ankles and even in the dim light behind the scenes the silver spangles gleamed against the scarlet of her dress.

"Come along!" she cried over her gleaming shoulder.

Seated before the triple mirrors of her dressing room, and in the pitiless glare of a dozen unshaded lights, Miss Scheff spoke frankly of the life of the stage.

Says She Hate It

"I hate it," she said, "it is nothing but work, work, work. Time goes flying by from week to week, from month to month. When it's Monday I wish it was Saturday; when Saturday comes, I wish it was Monday. I don't know why, but stage life makes you restless, restless.

"It's no life for a woman. I know that now. I didn't realize it years ago when I started. I couldn't understand why my parents opposed the idea of my going on the stage, but I know now. You bet I know!

"If I had my life to live over again I would not choose the stage—nearly anything but that.

"Look here, I'll tell you the truth about myself. I'll answer your questions. I went on the stage to sing in grand opera. I left grand opera for light opera and musical comedy. My first big hit was in 'Mlle. Modiste,' and I became well known because I would play on the drum! Ah! That's fame! What do you think of that? The play was nothing worth remembering. It was a popular success and it made me valuable to managers. I had no struggles, none of the usual difficulties that actresses tell about in interviews. I made good from the start.

"Oh yes, you are going to say that success brought me happiness. It never has, except in a way. If fame means being pointed out in the street by men you pass—well! That's not what I want.

"You hear a lot of the lure of applause. There's little in that, except that it means that the audience likes you. Naturally any actress likes that, because it means that she is successful and that her work is going over. But that is all it means! After nine or ten years on the stage it is all a part of the game.

Greatest Struggle Now

"I made good without an effort. But my efforts came later on. My greatest struggle is going on now. I'm keeping up. I'm holding my audiences. But one must struggle to do it.

"On the stage the years seem longer than in any other profession. Because a woman has been on the stage for a dozen years she is considered old. You realize that. People say: 'What? Fritzi Scheff? She must be awfully old now!' Look at me! Am I old? Answer me that."

There in the glare of those brilliant lights Fritzi leaned over, presenting her face for close inspection. It's true that she was garishly painted for the stage lights, but under the paint the flesh was firm and smooth. There are no wrinkles about the eyes or mouth, and even that little tell-tale wrinkle beneath the ear is missing. Fritzi appears to be in her twenties.

"And my voice! It's as good as it ever was. I never had a great voice. I never was a Galli-Curci, but I could sing, and I can still sing as well as ever. And I still draw audiences as well as I ever did.[32]

Has No Illusions

"You see, I haven't any illusion about the stage. It's my business. It's my way of making a living. But don't think that I like it. I don't.

"I never advise girls to go on the stage. And, goodness knows I've had an easier life than most actresses. The short time on the stage is only a part of it; it's the traveling, the time you waste, the time that you can do nothing. Then there's the tedious making up, and the waiting, waiting, waiting to go on. Now I am appearing twice a day. I haven't time to do anything else.

"And all I want is to be at home. I have a place in the country and I like to work in the garden. I like the cows and chickens, and I like to plant beans and cabbages and watch them grow. And look at me! Spangles, ribbons, velvet and lace. I wink, I am devilish, because the audience likes it. And what I want is to work in a garden! Ha!

"If I had a daughter I should hate to see her go on the stage, not for moral reasons or any of those old-fashioned notions, but simply because the artificial life is a deadly bore. But if I had a daughter I shouldn't try to influence her about it. I made my choice against my parents' wishes, and I can appreciate what a girl feels about the stage. But I'll tell you, I'd rather see a daughter of mine do almost anything else!"

Times-Picayune, April 5, 1922, p. 17.

EDITOR'S NOTE: FRIEDERIKE "FRITZI" Scheff was born in 1879 in Vienna, Austria-Hungary and died in 1954 after a long career on stage and screen.

16

THE WOOD CARVER

Finds Happiness in Shop

Choosing a Vocation

Wood Carver of Vieux Carré Finds Greatest Interest in Making Beautiful Things for Men Who Appreciate Them—Work Requires Special Talent, Says Henry Marinozzi

To those who know Royal street, any description of Marinozzi, the little Neapolitan wood carver, will be superfluous—for he has been there for the last eighteen years in his shop near Toulouse street.

The shop is very large and Marinozzi is very small, and he seems even smaller surrounded as he is with huge pieces of carved furniture. For carving is his life work and he is never idle. In fact, just now he has more work than he can do and the shop is piled high with antique pieces which are to be repaired, carved or "done over," as the case may be.

And he is a picturesque figure Although he has been in this country for twenty years, he is still typically Italian and he has all the fire of his race. More than one rich customer has been sent packing because she offended him by some impolite remark; for Marinozzi has a temperament. You bet he has!

A piece of fine furniture is something to be admired, petted, taken care of, says Marinozzi. You must treat it with respect.

I remember the first time I ever saw him – some ten years ago. He was talking to a woman from Boston, a tourist. She was a very elegant person, overdressed, commanding. She was regarding a large, carved bookcase through a lorgnette, and Marinozzi, in his shirt-sleeves, stood by her.

"A very fine piece," said the lady from Boston, condescendingly. Marinozzi smiled. "I make him myself," he said, flicking a piece of the cloth against one of the carved doors and looking highly pleased.

"But," the lady temporized, "it is much too large. It would never go into my apartment. Haven't you something smaller—something more delicate?"

"Bah!" cried Marinozzi. "No! I will not make a smaller one. It is that or nothing. They don't make houses to fit my furniture nowadays!"

And he promptly turned his back and went on with his carving, leaving the woman from Boston gasping.

When she recovered her breath she stalked out, but Marinozzi never even glanced up from his work.

But, like all fine workers, he has his own trade. Not only do men and women come to him from all sections of the city, but he ships his carvings to all parts of the United States.

Walk in some afternoon and talk to him. If you have an interest in the finer sort of wood carving he will always stop and talk, pointing out this or that fine detail.

"It is the designing that pleases me most," he says as he looks up from his work bench. "That is what I like. But no! I can't do that all the time. I must work, work!"

Henry Marinozzi learned his work in Italy. He and his brother

Raphael went to Casanova's Institute in Naples. When he was a young man Henry decided to come to America, but Raphael remained behind. Today Raphael Marinozzi is an officer in the Italian navy and Henry has his shop in Royal street, New Orleans.

But Henry Marinozzi has no regrets. He married a New Orleans girl, liked the South and remained. And he has been in Frenchtown for nearly twenty years.

Making beautiful things for people who appreciate them is the finest thing in the world he says. And he asks no more.

If you had a son, would you bring him up as a wood carver?" you ask.

Marinozzi shrugs his shoulders: "Who can say? I have no son—but, if I had, I should let him do what he wanted to. You cannot be an artist unless you have the talent. And my work is that of an artist. You must have talent for it."

But he has found the work he enjoys most—and that is enough he says.

Times-Picayune, April 13, 1922, p. 3.

Editor's Note: *Henry Marinozzi was a good friend of Saxon and he made appearances in a number of earlier news articles by the author.*

17

THE HOTEL MANAGER

His Work Demands Brains

Choosing a Vocation

Manager of St. Charles Hotel, Who Began Career as Bell-Hop in Toronto, Says That His Business Is One for Young Men of Brains and Ambition—Work Arduous But Worthwhile

Wasn't it the White Queen in "Through the Looking Glass" who advised Alice to try to believe six impossible things every morning before breakfast? "You have no idea how much practice counts in matters of this kind," she said.

The White Queen's advice came to my aid when Alfred Amer, manager of the St. Charles Hotel, said he began his career as a bell hop although I'll admit it's pretty hard to believe even when Mr. Amer assures you, with a smile, that it is true.

Today Mr. Amer is so much the suave, polished, assured man-of-the-world that it takes a big twist of imagination to think of him as a youngster in uniform, running from hotel lobbies at the call of "Front!" Nor can you imagine him chasing down corridors carrying the inevitable pitcher of ice water.

"Yes," said Mr. Amer, looking up from a letter he was writing, "I ran away from home to go into the hotel business. And I've never regretted it. I'd do it over again, because I believe that this business is one of the greatest in the world.

"Why, just think of it! We provide a home for men and women—not a mere shelter, but a real home, with everything running, night and day, on schedule time. This business is the composite of many businesses; not only the rooms, and the service, but our hotel, and every first class hotel is a unit in itself. We have our own electric plant, our own laundry, mechanics, upholsterers, carpenters, bakery, kitchen. We supply baths, massage, barber shops; we sell books and magazines, candy, cigars—there's no end to it.

Room for Ideas

"The management of it is the most interesting thing you can think of. You can use all your ideas, all your imagination, all the time.

"I find it fascinating, and I can think of nothing that would please me more than to see my son follow me in the business. But of course, he must decide that for himself. I realize that, because my father was determined that I should go into the wholesale drygoods business, his own line of work.

"That was in Toronto, Canada, and I was a youngster of 16 or 17. A friend of mine was a hotel clerk, and I thought that he was the finest man in the world. He lived at the hotel, you see, was always immaculate, well dressed. He took his meals in the hotel restaurant. Oh, he was a fine fellow. I thought the life was one of the greatest in the world, at any rate it was the life for me.

"So," and Mr. Amer laughed, "I ran away from home, if you can call it running away, because I landed a job as a bell-hop in the Rossin House right in Toronto. My father was very angry. He used to come into the lobby of the hotel where I worked in uniform and he would not even speak to me. It seems amusing now but it wasn't so funny in those days. We were both determined and neither one of us would give up our ideas.

Possible for Others

"Then I was promoted and went up and up. There's no use going into that, but after a time I found myself as one of the managers of the Waldorf in New York. Yes, it was a long way from bell-hop in the Rossin House, but what I did is possible for other ambitious boys or young men.

"In 1910 I came to New Orleans to the St. Charles Hotel, and I've been here ever since. That's really all there is to my story."

He was silent for a moment, then continued: "I'll tell you another reason why I like my business, it's the magnitude, the scope of it. Do you know that this business ranks fourth, as far as capital invested goes? And then, we deal in comfort, in protection, in helpfulness.

"The work, while arduous has rewards which are well worth while and it is worth all the thought you can put upon it. Of course I advocate thorough education for young men, but after their college course I think that the hotel business is a splendid one for the man with brains and ambition."

Mr. Amer is a member of the Advisory Council of the American Hotel Association and a member of the Southern Interstate Hotel Association. And his advice is worth listening to.

Times-Picayune, July 31, 1922, p. 5.

Editor's Note: *Alfred S. Amer also served on the Board of the French Opera House before it burned in 1919. It is likely that this flattering profile was part of Saxon's efforts to recruit influential people for his campaign to preserve and restore New Orleans architecture.*

18

THE SCULPTOR

Find Joy in Beautiful

Choosing a Vocation

Creation of Beautiful Things Gives Lasting Joy to Work, Says John Lachin, Sculptor and Modeler, Who Learned His Art in Venice—Is Teaching Sculpture at Arts Club.

The workshop is large and high, and through the large glass skylight the sun pours in, reflecting upon huge white urns, statues, columns and bowls. The air is moist with the dampness of drying clay and a fine film of gold-colored dust hangs in a bar of sunlight which crosses the workroom and falls upon the sculptured head of a cherub lying against the wall.

Workmen in overalls, their arms covered with the dazzling white of the plaster, move about at their tasks among the white columns and the sculptured figures. And John Lachin, standing in the center of the square of sunlight, leans upon a white satyr's head, part of a group in which a nymph is pursued ceaselessly, but never clasped, as upon the Grecian urn.

John Lachin is a Venetian. He was born somewhere near the Doge's palace on the Grand canal. He spent his childhood in the workshop of his father, a sculptor. His earliest recollections are of the graven figures on the facades of the buildings at the water's edge.

It was more than natural—it was almost inevitable that the boy should follow his father's art and make it his own. He was still a very young man when, with his father and his younger brother, Victor, he came to New Orleans.

Son to Learn Art

For sixteen years the Lachins have been here. John Lachin continued his training in the studio of Pietro Ghiloni. Today, Mr. Lachin has a large studio and workshop of his own at 527 Toulouse street. His father and his brother are associates with him. Soon his son will learn sculpture from his father, just as John and Victor learned from their father in Italy.

Of course the business is not confined to sculpture alone, in fact most of the work is decorative, ceilings, cornices, fireplaces and the various types of decorations used by architects and interior decorators.

Many of the theaters, public buildings and fine residences of New Orleans show examples of the work of the Lachins: the Elks' lodge-room ceiling of plaster and caen-stone; the decorations on the Benjamin house in upper St. Charles avenue; the Dreyfus residence and many of the churches and schools.

"But it is modeling in clay which pleases me the most!" said Mr. Lachin as he stood by the satyr's head in his studio. "There is a satisfaction in modeling which I find interests me more than any other type of my work. That's why I am so interested in the work of the Arts and Crafts Club in Royal street. I think that organization is doing and will do a great good here. It presents a real opportunity to the gifted boy and girl to get first-class training without expense."

Conducts Free Classes

Mr. Lachin conducts the class in sculpture each Tuesday night at the Arts Club, free of charge. He is donating his service, giving his knowledge to the students; and this is the knowledge which has taken him all his life to learn.

"If you had your life to live over again, would you choose sculpture?" he was asked.

He smiled and his black eyes twinkled: "What do you think?" he parried, "I am bringing up my son as I was brought up"

"What part of your work interests you most?"

"This!" said Mr. Lachin, showing a sample of scratched ornament —very beautiful raised ornamentation along a cornice. "It is called 'sgraffito' and to me it is the most interesting thing in the world. I'm always happiest when I am working upon something beautiful.

"No, there is no question about it—if I were reliving my life, I would do just as I have done."

And his brother, Victor, standing by nodded in assent.

Times-Picayune, April 19, 1922, p. 6.

19

THE KEEPER OF LIGHT

UNUSUAL WAYS OF MAKING A LIVING

Beacon in the Heart of the City is Made to Burn for Those Far Down the River in Ships.

We all know the light which burns nightly in the high tower above the city.

From every quarter men look toward it and speak of it. Little old women in the French Quarter, who have not left their homes in years, can see it from their balconies, and on warm nights they sit and gaze at this symbol of the new New Orleans, standing high above the fantastic skyline of the Vieux Carré.

Sailors from foreign ports, sitting of an evening in Jackson Square, speak of the light, pointing toward it with outstretched arms; it was the first thing that they could see as they approached the city—and it will be the last which they will see as the city fades from view when they go away.

For the light in the Hibernia Bank building tower is a chartered lighthouse of the United States government, and sends its cheering message far down the Mississippi toward the Gulf. Mariners say it can be seen for sixty miles.

From the gardens far in the uptown district, little children point toward the light in the evening; travelers approaching the city upon trains can see it long before the city itself comes into view.

Yes, we all know this light which shines nightly in the tower, and we accept it along with the sun and the rain. Even in a short time it has become a part of things, to be taken along with the rest. And few of us have thought of the keeper of the light—for a keeper there must be, a man to tend the light, to watch it, to see that it ever burns.

If you will go to the top of the tower, almost any afternoon, you will find him, making his tour of inspection in the room above the colonnade in that small circular room atop the battlements. John Jacquet is his name, a man of forty, quiet in speech, and all his interest centered on the light.

He will show you the little platform in the top of this room, from which an iron ladder leads up still higher—35 feet higher—into the shaft which runs to the apex of the building. It is at the top of this small circular shaft that the light swings in a basket, behind the curving glass of the lantern. In the basket there are two 500-watt incandescent globes, protected by two 10-ampere fuses on the 21st floor.

You inquire the reason for two lights, and he smiles:

"Well, you see," he says, "there must always be one light in the tower, of course, as this is a lighthouse—and one of them might have an accident. They can be lowered down the shaft on a chain. That saves climbing up the ladder every day. It's not as easy as it looks—climbing that ladder. Of course, I must go up three times a week in order to clean the inside of the glass in the lantern, but on the other days, the lights are lowered for inspection.

"Let's see—35 feet to climb three times a week. Why in a year I'll have climbed 5460 feet! Sounds like an altitude record, doesn't it?"

But there is other work as well, for the lights which illuminate the tower from the outside must be kept clean. They must be examined daily and the necessary changes of globes made. In stormy weather this is quite a task as they are all on exposed portions of the tower.

But Mr. Jacquet is tremendously interested in his work. From his house in St. John's Court near Bayou St. John, his wife can see the shining tower, and looking across the intervening space of an evening, she knows that her husband is working there at his task as keeper of the light.

Times-Picayune, July 26, 1922, p. 12.

Editor's Note: *Before John A. Jacquet took the Lighthouse tender job, he retired from his former profession as a machinist for the city railroad. He was born in France around 1856 and immigrated to the US in 1872. Jacquet was about sixty-four years old at the time of this interview.*

20

THE LADY LOCKSMITH

UNUSUAL WAYS OF MAKING A LIVING

A Woman Takes Up the Work of Opening Locks Where Her Husband Left Off.

"Me? A female Raffles? Oh, No!"[33]

Mrs. Josephine Duble Miller, the lady locksmith of Commercial Alley, looked up from her work bench and laid down her chisel.

"I suppose I could be a good burglar if I wanted to," she mused as she toyed with a large iron key, "but it's not being done this season! Not by me, at least!"

She smiled: "From the experience I've had, burglary ought to be child's play for me, if I ever decide to take it up. But seriously, though, I've been sixteen years in this shop—sixteen years at the bench—and locks, after you get to know 'em, are as simple as your A B C's.

Unusual Ways of Making a Living
BY LYLE SAXON
No. 2—The Lady Locksmith.
A Woman Takes Up the Work of Opening Locks Where Her Husband Left Off.

Illustration 7. *Unusual Ways of Making a Living No. 2. The Lady Locksmith.* Times-Picayune, *July 27, 1922, p. 5.*

"When I married Mr. Duble, I used to sit here in the shop and watch him work. The locks and keys fascinated me After I had been watching him at work for a year and a half, I decided I'd like to try it. So I began. He taught me everything I know. My first job was a success, and I felt encouraged.

"One afternoon—I remember it as though it were yesterday—my husband had a slight hemorrhage. It terrified me. He had been sick for some time, and that day he had done unusually hard work. He was sitting in a chair just inside the door so weak that he could hardly stand.

"I spoke to him: 'You ought to be at home, in bed—' I was beginning when a man came rushing in. He was all excited. A desk must be opened at once, he said. It simply had to be opened that night. My husband wanted to go, but he was too weak. I began taking off my apron. 'I'll go,' I said. 'It won't hurt for me to try.'

"My husband laughed at me, sick as he was. He said I could never do it, but I was determined that he shouldn't lose that job. Well, to make a long story short, I went and I opened that desk, too. It was a long trip for the house was somewhere near the Barracks, down at Chalmette, I remember.

"I came home late, but I was happy because I had opened up that lock without any difficulty at all."

She paused for a moment, brushing up a lock of hair which had fallen across her forehead:

"So I kept on after that," she said, "and when my husband died, I continued to run the business. The longer I work at locks, the better I like them. For instance, look at this. Here's a problem!"

She held out her hand. There, lying across her palm, was an antique lock of hand-hammered brass; it was simple enough in its mechanism, but the key was lost, and it was the key which she was making. It was a problem indeed, for the head of the key—that part which fits into the lock—was in the design of a four-leafed clover.

"Of course, it must be done entirely by hand," said Mrs. Miller. "Some job, too.

"But this is the kind of work I like—something different.

"You'd be surprised," she went on, "at the kind of work that turns up. Why, not long ago I was called to the old St. Louis Cemetery in a great hurry. One of the old family vaults was locked and the key was lost. It had to be opened for a funeral. Well, I went and had it open in no time. I didn't enjoy that job much though."

"Do you have many emergency calls?" she was asked,

"Oh, yes," she said. "Hardly a day passes that I don't have to go into some home or office to open a locked door or a locked desk or trunk. You'd be surprised to know how many places there are that get locked up—nobody seems to know how or why. But they all must be opened again. Yes, I'm kept busy. It's fun sometimes, going to try your hand where other locksmiths have failed. It puts you on your mettle—gets you all keyed up, you might say!" And she laughed.

Times-Picayune, July 27, 1922, p. 5.

21

THE COBBLER-PAINTER

Unusual Ways of Making a Living

A Shoemaker, Turning to Art, Paints Pictures in Lafayette Square for All Who'll Buy.

~

Who said art didn't pay?

Not J.J. Sutherland the painter of Lafayette square, for he turned to art when his trade of shoemaking failed him. And he is making a living.

Not a luxurious living, of course—but then, what can a man expect to make when he sells his finished product for 35 cents? Not a fortune, certainly. Perhaps, if he were able to manufacture them by wholesale lots, he might. But a painter cannot do that; it takes time, you know, lots of time.

Any afternoon, should you walk through the square, you will find him on one of the iron benches, somewhere near the statue of Henry Clay; and you will find him hard at work. As the shadow of the statue lengthens, the brush moves more rapidly—for the night is coming, as the song says, and man's work is done. Color is tricky, you know, and artificial light is difficult. The things you paint by candlelight seldom seem the same by day. Art is long—and time is fleeting. You bet it is! Yessir!

Mr. Sutherland is 63 years old, and he never painted "professionally" he says, until this summer—although he has dabbled in color since 1880, and has sold some of his enlargements from photographs for as much as $25. But that was good luck—and his luck has changed. Painting used to be an amusement, a hobby—something to take his mind away from his cobbler's last. Then came the hard times. There was no more work to be had. He tried shop after shop in New Orleans. It was a hard business too, getting around, for he is lame.

Sold Three First Day

When his money was exhausted, there was nothing left to do but to paint. For years he had done it for his own amusement, and many persons had stopped to admire. Why not try to sell them? So he went to Lafayette Square. If he priced them cheaply enough, he reasoned, there would be buyers.

"Of course, I can't make much with this," he said, as he laid aside a small masterpiece in which snow white dogs chased each other across arsenic green meadows and baby-blue lakes reflected the deeper sapphire of the sky with surprising accuracy, "but 35 cents is 35 cents!"

There was no denying this.

He turned over several other pictures. There was a general impression of vivid landscapes in which horses and cows romped playfully, peaceful churches and storms at sea gathered in friendly proximity.

"Do you always paint fanciful pictures or do you sometimes paint the things you see around you?" he was asked.

He seemed perplexed for a moment, then exclaimed: "Why I've seen all these things! As I go about the country, I watch, and when I see something I like, I remember it. Then I paint two or three things that I like into one picture. Simple enough, and a good way, too!"

Men, he says, are the greatest buyers of his works of art; women come to look and admire, but they seldom buy. But he has a following in Lafayette Square—you'd be surprised.

Gets Many Compliments

"I work here nearly all day," he continued, "and the men come and sit near me and watch me work. I get lots of compliments. And many of them would buy from me, too, if they had the money. Oh yes, you learn something about human nature, sitting in a public park all day.

"There are two little bootblacks who save their nickels to buy my pictures. I let 'em go even cheaper than my usual price, because the kids like 'em so much. They come and watch me every day, and they pay for their pictures 5 cents at a time. I don't know what they do with them, but each of the boys has bought two paintings. Really, I'd like to know. I believe I'll ask 'em!"

Some days, Mr. Sutherland has good luck and makes as much as $3—but on other days his sales fall off to a dollar or less. The average, he says, is about $1.50 a day. And in rainy weather—nothing. Nobody buys, nobody. Really it's no use to sit in the square.

Anyway, he's thinking of trying City Park. He thinks he might do better there. He's going to try it for a while. Maybe he will go out Sunday and try his luck. The swans in the lagoon will furnish a fine subject. If you just add some other things to make the background interesting.

For the present he is living at 700 Camp street with an old shoemaker—a friend of his.

Times-Picayune, July 28, 1922, p. 11.

22

THE BALLOON MAN

Unusual Ways of Making a Living

Seller of Colored Bubbles Has Irresistible Fascination for Children

~

Have you ever attended a band concert in one of the New Orleans parks at sunset on a summer's afternoon?

If you have, you have noticed the balloons—hundreds of colored bubbles, bobbing about in the air above the crowd. And each balloon is held by a happy youngster, who sits there delighted with his treasure.

For the balloon man is the child's first affinity. There is something fascinating about the man—that dark stranger who holds a hundred captive globes of color in his hands; the man who appears out of nowhere with his treasures, disposes of them and disappears as mysteriously as he came. It's like magic, like Santa Claus and the Easter Rabbit—oh, that balloon man is a fine fellow. All the children love him.

It seems a pity that we grow too old and too dignified to enjoy balloons ourselves; but we never grow too old to enjoy watching them in the hands of children. They, luckily, have no such conventional standards to maintain, and a red balloon is their rightful property. And it is an unusual child who does not demand one as the vendor appears.

The Pied Piper of Hamelin finds his parallel today in the balloon man. For he caters exclusively to children. They follow him anywhere.

John Lella, who lives in a cottage at 909 North Derbigny street, is the balloon man of Audubon Park. His little house is a veritable treasure trove for children. There are whole trays of balloons; sad looking bits of colored rubber, but they will swell and swell when they are filled with gas—and a small handful makes a large bunch when inflated.

There are other things, too. Hundreds of tiny tissue-paper parasols, fit for the hands of a fairy. They open and close, just as the large ones do. And one is guaranteed to make any little girl happy, for a time at least—but woe betide her if she is caught in a summer shower! For the little parasol will disappear in her hands—gone in a flash!

Lella makes the little parasols himself, and his wife and children help him. For a time he maintained a small factory in Bourbon street, but he found that it didn't pay.

Lella has other things, too. He manufactures tiny monkeys, made of fine wire wound in spirals, attached to a head molded of red clay, glazed over. The monkeys hang upon strings and a touch of the hand sends them into a spasm of ecstasy; they never cease their quivering. They seem strangely alive.

Making them is quite a task, for the modeling of the head requires time and patience; then the hair must be attached; after that, the process is simpler. The coils of wire for the arms, body and head are attached, and a tiny American flag is affixed in one hand to give a festive touch. Then they are attached to strings and they are ready for the street.

Lella takes an artist's pride in his work. He has just invented another toy—strangely like the monkey—which he says will delight the children, if his own are judges. This is a red devil, with a pitchfork which he brandishes when the string is set in motion. It is ugly enough to scare a child into spasms, but, strangely enough, the children accept this comical fellow with glee.

But balloons sell best. Lella has been selling them for twenty-two years, ever since the day he landed in America, an emigrant from Italy. He began peddling them on Riverside Drive in New York. Nine years ago he came to New Orleans.

Children cannot resist them, he says. They sell themselves.

Little girls like the paper parasols because they are novelties, and little boys like the monkeys—but neither can touch the balloon for popularity. It has been popular ever since Lella can remember—and will be, he says, long after the monkeys and the parasols have been superseded by other toys.

The fascination of the balloon, he says, is demonstrated by his own children, who have never tired of them, although they see hundreds every day.

On Sundays you will see him in Audubon Park, followed by a crowd of children, and on week days he has a small stand at Canal and Bourbon streets. In the late afternoons and at night he works with his toys, manufacturing new ones, duplicating the old. For there is a large demand—and there will always be, he says, as long as there are children in the world.

Times-Picayune, July 29, 1922, p. 5.

23

THE MAKER OF STATUES

Unusual Ways of Making a Living

The Biagis Make Plaster Saints and Gild Them, for Any Shrine

Down in Chartres street, near the cathedral, is the workshop of the Biagis, who spend their time making plaster saints. Their workroom is a long, low chamber, running from the sidewalk to one of the most beautiful courtyards in the Vieux Carré—the "court of the vine," so called because a gnarled grape vine covers the walls, and drapes its green festoons across the court from chimney to chimney.

On warm, sunny days the Biagis take their statues into the court, and work there. Almost any summer day you will find them, bending over their statues, applying the brilliant colors—Reds, blues, yellows and decorations of gold-leaf.

The name of the firm is "J. Biagioni, L. Biagi and Company," but it numbers at present, Joseph Biagi, Frank Adami and Leo Biagi.

Joseph is usually alone in the shop, while the others are out repairing broken statues, or repainting those whose colors have become dimmed, even in the half-light of church naves.

Joseph is the typical Italian, pleasant, suave and tremendously interested in his work. As he applies the gold-leaf to a saint's halo he will tell you of his career.

It began when he was a child in Italy. He and his brothers were all interested in sculpture, and they learned their trade with an old Italian. Nine years ago they came to America, went to Chicago and worked with the Daprato Statuary Company—probably the largest makers of religious statues in the country. Then the brothers came to New Orleans and opened their workroom in Chartres street. They have been there ever since.

In the Catholic churches of the city you will find their handiwork. Many of the churches have been decorated by them—but they are proudest of St. Joseph's Academy in Ursuline avenue, which they decorated entirely, and for which they furnished all the statues.

It seems odd to a layman—for when you sit in a darkened church and gaze at the lifelike images which set in niches in the walls, it seems that they are a part of the edifice itself. But, like human beings, time brings the marks of age, and once in a while the saints must be removed and given a fresh coat of paint. Then they are returned to their places.

The Chartres street workroom is rather a disconcerting place, for one sits in proximity with all the saints of the calendar, saints whose eyes regard you sadly, following you about as you move from place to place.

You pause uncertainly before a life-size statue in a corner. His eyes seem alive, no matter how closely you peer.

"Why do his eyes follow you so?" you ask, almost in a whisper—lowering your voice as is proper when speaking of religious matters.

"Glass eyes, that's why!" says Joseph laughing at your amazement. "They cost ten dollars extra—they're regular glass eyes, just as people use."

After this, you are not so intimidated by the plaster saints, and you continue your investigations. A large figure stands, covered with a heavy cloth. "May I look?" you ask.

"Sure!" says Joseph Biagi.

You pull the cloth, and it falls off suddenly, disclosing, to your startled gaze, a life-sized statue of St. Anthony – but, wonder of wonders—he is a negro! A rich coffee-colored face, an expression of deep sadness—and one of his brown hands raised in admonition. You are speechless before this. But Joseph reassures you.

"He is the black St. Joseph," says Biagi. We made him for the negro church in Tulane avenue—St. Catherine's Church. I do not know his history, but it was done for a special order. It is a very popular saint with the colored people of New Orleans, they tell me. He works miracles."

What strange saint is this? You wonder, remembering a black virgin that you saw once, a statue taken from some European shrine. You ask further questions but Biagi cannot answer.

"Go out and see the statue anytime," he says. "It stands in the church, as I say. Maybe the priest can tell you. Ask him."

And he turns to other saints. There are hundreds of models. Saint Rita is a popular favorite, with Saint Raymond and Saint Aloysius coming next.

"These statues must exert a good influence upon you," you say, as Biagi shows you a whole room full of the waxy white forms, which have not received their paint as yet. He shrugs: "Perhaps!" he says.

But then you realize the truth of the matter. The statues, after all, are only statues. Their religious significance comes only through the attitude of mind in which they are regarded in churches, or in private shrines. After all, they are only plaster and water, and a little coloring.

And yet, they are more than that. They represent careful work, careful consideration, and reverence. For Joseph Biagi is reverent. Naturally, the proximity with all these statues, and the fact that he creates them himself, has robbed them of their aloofness—but, for all that, the finished product is treated with proper respect.

It is not, Biagi explains, that the clay and plaster means anything itself, but the finished statue represents something. He has respect for that—Oh yes!

The statue is a symbol.

Times-Picayune, July 31, 1922, p. 5.

EDITOR'S NOTE: *Joseph Biagi arrived in the United States from Italy in 1907 and became an American citizen in 1918. Sometime after this interview, he moved to the Lower Garden District of New Orleans where he opened his own fine art studio.*

24

THE LEGLESS NEWSBOY

Unusual Ways of Making a Living

Victim of Train Accident Finds Selling Papers Better Than Being Dependent Upon Others

No doubt you have seen Wilhelm Muller. He sits at a small table at St. Charles and Poydras streets and sells papers. He is there every day, rain or shine, hot or cold.

There is nothing unusual, of course, in the fact that he sells papers for a living, but when you think of the obstacles which he has overcome—well, there's your story.

The part of Muller which shows above the table's edge is that of a normal middle-aged man, but the part which shows is all there is—there isn't any more.

"I was always an active man," he says, smiling at you, as you lean upon the table where the daily papers are weighted down by horse-shoes. "I came to America from the old country—from Germany. I was a sailor, and I had been a sailor ever since I was a boy. Trip after trip I made to New Orleans—and I liked it here.

"You hear a lot of the call in the sea, but I didn't like it. When I was sailing in northern seas, I would think about New Orleans, where it was always warm and green—know what I mean? I used to get homesick for it, and I decided to quit the sea and get a job here.

"So I did. That is, I quit the sea, but the job I managed to land was in Mississippi, near Wiggins. I worked only one day.

"That night a wagon in which I was riding was struck by a railroad train. The others were killed and my legs were mangled. They took me to a hospital and amputated both of them above the knee. But I didn't get better, and the doctor said it was gangrene; so they operated again. This time they cut off both legs almost at the hips. I got better then.

"The railroad paid me $2000 for the accident. One thousand for each leg doesn't seem like much, does it? But it was all I got.

"Lying in bed I used to wonder what I was going to do. I thought about all the wrecks I had seen in the streets—men without legs or arms, beggars, you know. I'd always made a living, and lying there, I swore that I'd never beg.

"When I got out of the hospital I had the $2000 and I thought I'd give it to some home for incurables, or some home for cripples, and they'd let me live there for the rest of my life. I did try that, but it didn't work. I gave $500 to a house of that kind—there's no good in calling names now—but I found I couldn't stay. I thought I'd get out and try working at something. I didn't want to be dependent.

"The shock, or the operation or something, had made me deaf, so that was another obstacle. But I found that I could get around on a sort of wagon—a little three-wheeled cart, which I could push with my hands. I had one made, and learned to ride on it, keeping my balance and going ahead at the same time. The rough streets hurt my hands, so I had a couple of wooden grips made—just like stirrups, with metal on the outside. By holding these and pushing along I could make fairly good time.

"After I found a means of getting around things were easier. I began by selling pencils and gum, but I didn't like that. Then I began selling papers. I stayed in New Orleans for a while, and then thought I'd try Chicago.

"Say! Have you ever spent a winter in that town? Cold! Oh, gee! I nearly died. My deafness got worse and I could hardly hear a thing. I had to sit in the streets in order to sell my papers and I could feel myself freezing. I got sick. I got homesick, too. I kept thinking about New Orleans, where it was always warm and green. I told you about that feeling before, didn't I?

"Finally, I came back. That was two years ago. I opened my stand here on this corner, and I've been here ever since. I don't think I'll ever go away again. I'm making a living, getting along. I don't owe any man a dime, not a cent. I pay my board and lodging and manage to put a little by for my old age.

"I'm not exactly a young man now, you know. I'm 40; I was 31 when I lost my legs. I'm sort of used to it now, although I can't say I'm resigned exactly. I still miss 'em.

"But you know, I've got a horror of those fellows who try to beg a living by making folks feel for 'em. That's why I sit at a table that covers me from the waist down. I guess that some of 'em would get a shock if they looked under the table and saw that I wasn't there at all! I just sort of stop at the waist.

I'll bet there are lots of my customers who don't know that I'm two legs short. And I've got lots of steady customers.

"Things are pretty slow just now, but I'm getting along. And I'm going to keep on working as long as I can.

"Well, so long! Glad to have seen you! Stop by again some time!"

Times-Picayune, August 1, 1922, p. 5.

25

THE PARK PHOTOGRAPHER

Unusual Ways of Making a Living

Camera Man in City Park is Always Surrounded by Large Crowd of Children

Any sunny afternoon you will find him in City Park, his camera beside him, surrounded always by a crowd of laughing children. Wolf Rosensweig is his name, and he has been the park photographer for nine years. He has been there, in fact, ever since he came to America from Russia, seeking a new home, and leaving behind him the flour mills of Odessa where he had toiled since childhood.

"And even now, to this day, I wake up in the night to think how glad I am that I came to America!" he says.

Rosensweig is a philosopher; he has thought about life, and he has modeled his own life to fit his philosophy.

"We work, we sleep, we eat and we spend some time resting," he said, as he settled himself on a bench near the children's wading pool in the shadow of the great oak trees. "Back in Russia I used to think about those things, and I decided what I wanted to do. That's why I came to this country; I wanted to find my own sort of life. And I found it right here."

His gesture included the surrounding park, the children splashing in the pool, the mothers and nurses on benches. "I like to see people happy," he continued. "I like to make pictures of happy people. Often men have come to me and said: 'Why don't you do something that will bring you more money?' But I know what I want, and I stay right here. I could make more money in a factory, I suppose, or working at something else. But what's the use of that? I like this; I don't like a factory. I make enough money to get along; I don't need much—you'd be surprised how little I do need. And by Golly; I like to watch the children playing. They're better than a picture show.

I've always liked children, little children. I'm an old bachelor and maybe that's the reason. What you think?"

He laughed, but it was a friendly laugh; there was no cynicism there.

"All day long I laugh at them. All day long I watch them. Sometimes I make money in a day—one, two, three, four, five dollars. Other days nothing. When it is dark, nothing. When it rains, nothing. But I make a living. This is a bad year, the worst that I've seen since I came to the park. They say to me: Ain't you discouraged?' or 'Don't you want another job?' Ha! Not me! I'm satisfied with what I've got.

"Lots of men are never satisfied. They kick against the country or the government. You never hear me kick the United States. I remember the flour mills of Odessa.

"This country has treated me good, too! Do you know what I had when I came here? No? I'll tell you. I had a pair of patent leather boots, high Russian boots. I sold them for two dollars. What use were Russian leather boots to me in New Orleans, Ha! Tell me that?"

He looked out over the pool before him where children romped in the shallow water, and the sun, coming through the leaves of the oaks made a checkered shade. A broad beam of light fell on the fountain, turning the spray into a rainbow. Somewhere in the trees a bird was singing; and the long spirals of sad-colored moss moved lazily back and forth in the sunlit air.

More children were arriving. They came running with little shouts of laughter to the edge of the pool.

"Do you see that?" asked the camera man, "I stay here all day, every day. I never get tired of watching them. They all know me, and I have taken pictures of many of them. This is where I find happiness. Look! Understand me well. Some men work hard, all day; then they work again at night, in order to get just a little more money. They get no pleasure out of life. They are greedy; they want everything; but they get nothing. Me, I am different. I enjoy each day as it comes. I make a living and I manage to save a little. Every week there is a little to put by. I don't owe any man.

"Lots of people have more than I have—but what do I care? I have enough. Some day I'll die; you'll die; they'll all die. And in the meantime, what? A little work, a little pleasure, we eat and we sleep. I have lots of time to think about this. And you know that I wouldn't change places with any man alive!"

A group of children passed, stiff and starched in their pink and blue dresses. Their mother, walking beside them, spied the camera man:

"Come take our pictures!" she called.

The man rose from the bench and lifting the heavy camera to his shoulder, said goodbye. Then he followed the mother and the children through the shadows into the sunlight beyond the trees.

Times-Picayune, August 2, 1922, p. 5.

***Editor's Note:** Leo Wolf Rosensweig (1873-1951) was born in Russia and emigrated to the United States in 1900. Despite his abilities as a photographer, he was unable to read or write, and never learned those skills.*

26

THE STREET SINGER

UNUSUAL WAYS OF MAKING A LIVING

A Blind Youth Sings With a Vision of a Day When He Hopes to Be a Great Singer

~

Down in Chartres street, in the heart of the Vieux Carré, is a small coffee house frequented by sailors from the seven seas.

There is a free and easy air about the place, probably due, in part, to the large and roughly painted frescoes on the mouldering plaster walls between the heavy battened doors: Hula girls disporting themselves beneath palm trees which stand out boldly against a brilliant sky, painted, perhaps, by a sailor in remembrance of Hawaii or Tahiti or one of the other islands of the tropic seas.

Below this exotic decoration is an irregular group of marble-topped tables where men loll at ease, drinking their coffee or their beer, talking, or drowsing with heads pillowed on folded arms. The man who takes your order has stars and anchors tattooed on his hands, but the coffee is brought to you a moment latter by a bobbed-haired girl with an infectious grin and a fine line of freckles across the bridge of her tip-tilted nose.

A man speaks: "Give us a song, Gilbert!"

Unusual Ways of Making a Living
A Blind Youth Sings With a Vision of a Day When He Hopes to Be a Great Singer.

Illustration 8. *Unusual Ways of Making a Living No. 8. The Street Singer.* Times-Picayune, *August 3, 1922, p. 6.*

You look toward the speaker, a sailor, who has addressed a blind boy leaning back in his chair against the wall, cuddling his chin against the polished body of a guitar.

There comes a pause in the buzzing talk; all nationalities share the interest in music, it seems. The boy strikes a few random chords and begins to sing.

Voice Is a Surprise

And, sipping your coffee slowly, you listen.

The song is commonplace enough, a ballad, but the boy's voice is remarkable; it is untrained but rich, full and sweet, a high baritone. You listen while the coffee cools before you. He goes on and on, his voice rising higher and higher and higher. Will it break? You wonder. But it goes on triumphantly to the end, soaring to high C, and then dying away into a mere whisper of sound. The song is over and there is a spattering of applause. Then the men return to their coffee and their talk.

The ease of the blind singer's performance is remarkable; evidently, taking high C is a matter-of-fact, every-day affair with him, for he is singing his songs for the nickels and dimes which the men give him in this little cafe. As you look at him you remember that you have seen him singing in the streets on Sunday evenings, with another boy who plays the violin. Many others must have seen him and heard him, and you wonder that someone has not taken an interest in his voice.

But then! You did not notice it particularly yourself, when you heard him before—probably the noise of the street, or the type of song he was singing did not give his voice a chance. Surely, it is remarkable enough in this little cafe. You cross over and speak to him, and a moment later you are talking with him across one of the small marble-topped tables.

His name he tells you, is Gilbert Mestier, and he lives with his mother at 536 Chartres street, just next door to the coffee house. He has been blind for a long time and he has been singing ever since he was a child. Music was his natural mode of expression. Although totally without training, he has learned to play upon the guitar, the piano, the banjo, the cornet—almost any instrument, in fact. But, most of all, he likes to sing.

Sings with Cripple

He earns his living by singing in the streets with Teddy Miller, who has only one leg. Gilbert plays the guitar. Teddy the violin. Both of them sing. At other times Gilbert sings in the little cafe in Chartres street.

"I know I can sing—I know I can sing," he repeats over and over. "All I want is a chance. I'm sure I could amount to something if I had the training. That's what I want. I want to amount to something big. I want to be a great singer.

"I dream about it all the time. You may not believe me, but I swear it's the truth—I dream about Caruso. Yesterday I dreamed about him. I've never seen him, you know, and I've never heard him sing, except on a phonograph, but I saw him in my dream. He had on a long black robe with a cord tied around his waist. I went up to him and I said: 'Oh, let me learn how to sing,' and he put his arms around my waist and said: 'Yes, Gilbert.'

"In my dream I began to cry, but he said: 'Don't do that, it will hurt your voice.' And then I told him that I never smoked cigarettes or drank liquor because I wanted my voice to be fine and big and that I knew smoking and drinking hurt it. Then he told me that he was going to wash out my throat with a sort of rubber hose, so I could sing better. I woke up then. Funny, you know, but I dream all the time and it's always about singing. I wonder why it is?"

There was a little pause, and one of the men asked the boy to sing, but he was too intent on his story.

Thought He Was Cured

If I weren't blind I would work and make money for lessons," he continued, "but I'm blind and I can't work, except by singing like this. I don't make much this way, and I'm wearing out my voice. I ought not sing today, because I've got a cold.

"Once I thought I was cured of my blindness," he said, "but it was a mistake. Do you remember Brother Isaiah, the Miracle Man. I went to him and he tried to cure me. I shouldn't have gone, because I am a Catholic, and I should have stayed with my own church, but I went. Brother Isaiah was sure he could cure me, and I used to sing at his meetings. He asked me to come and live on his boat.

"I went, and I let my hair grow long, and worked all day, just like he told me to do. He used to pray over me every night and I would sing. I stayed with him for months—and for a while I thought I was better, but I wasn't. Finally I knew he couldn't cure me and I came home again. I'm right where I was before I went. I've sort of given up hope of being cured now, but I've got my voice and I'm going to succeed with that.

"I believe it as sure as I'm sitting here. Someday I'll get my chance. You never can tell. Maybe some millionaire will hear me sing and offer to give me lessons. It's the only thing in the world I want. I want to be a great singer. With the voice I've got, do you think I've got a chance?"

There is a moment's pause before you reply:

"Many singers have started with less," you answer.

Men's voices call to the blind boy: "Come on, sing for us! We're waiting for a song."

Obediently his fingers strike a random chord and he begins to sing.

Times-Picayune, August 3, 1922, p. 6.

Editor's Note: *Gilbert Mestier was born around 1907 in New Orleans. At the time of this interview he was fifteen years old.*

27

THE MAN WITH THE PARAKEETS

Unusual Ways of Making a Living

A Wand, a Cage and Seven Birds Are Entire "Stock in Trade" of a Man Who Sells an Occult Service

You have seen him often, of course—the man with the parakeets.

You can find him at Rampart and Canal street any afternoon, or any evening, standing beside his cage of brilliant green birds—birds which keep up a constant small chatter among themselves as they hop about the narrow cage.

For this cage is John Suozzo's entire capital stock, and it affords him a living—for these birds are seers and oracles—if you believe the sign which hangs above them:

"Ladies and gents! These birds will tell your fortune and future life by taking a planet. Children also!" and then, on a small metal disc is the mystic sign, "Ten Cents."

If you can withstand this, and loiter along with an undecided expression, he will fix you with his eye, and say, insinuatingly: "Let these innocent little birds tell your fortune?"

You part with the two nickels, and Suozzo proceeds to business. The cage door is opened, and he calls: Virginia!"

Virginia is a very small parakeet, very pert and saucy. She steps down from the perch and minces forth, hesitates for a moment, and finally, after making up her mind, selects a slip of pink paper from the tray which hangs before the cage. She then returns to her perch.

"Charley!" calls Suozzo.

Charley is a sad-looking bird with ruffled plumage; he walks sedately forth and picks up the paper which Virginia has abandoned, then mounting the wooden wand which Suozzo offers, he allows you to take the paper from his bill. Then he, like Virginia, returns to the perch.

Suozzo assures you that the paper which is given you will tell your past, present and future, so you open it forthwith.

"Planet of the fortune for a gentleman," it reads. "The star of your horoscope proclaims you are very fortunate"—so far so good—"If you have been unlucky the early part of your life, so much the better"—this is harder to believe, but you continue—"Some trouble will happen, but after it has passed, you will be lucky for the rest of your life." Ah! A sigh of relief. "Your wife is a great treasure to you; you will have twelve children." You spare me! "You will live about 81 years."

"If you don't like that, I'll have Pete get you another one," says Suozzo obligingly. But one "horoscope" is enough. You decline with thanks.

Then, if you talk with him, Suozzo will tell you something of his life with his parakeets. He has gone from state to state with them, and has even crossed the continent to attend the San Francisco exposition back in 1915. The birds have supported him for more than forty years. They are his best friends. Every one answers to his or her name, and to prove it, he will call them, each in turn:

"Virginia!" and the perky one appears. "Dick! Charley! Pete! Tommy! Felix!" Six little green birds are ranged on top of the cage, but one remains inside. "Mary!" he calls sharply, and she emerges, looking cross and ruffled.

"She's always the last one out!" says Suozzo. And then Mary fires a toy cannon to redeem herself, and the others climb ladders and drill like soldiers.

The eyes of John Suozzo shine with pride.

"What do you think of my children?" he asks.

Times-Picayune, August 4, 1922, p. 12.

***Editor's Note:** John Suozzo was born in Italy in 1854 and immigrated to the US in 1883. He and his wife Annie lived in the French Quarter on Dumaine Street near Burgundy.*

28

SHORTHAND AT 73

UNUSUAL WAYS OF MAKING A LIVING

Teaching Shorthand Is No Prosaic Existence to This Man Who Invents His Own Philosophy

Back in the days when you and I were young, Maggie, there was a crack stenographer in the civil district court under Judge Houston. His name was S.L. Polock, and it is said that he was a whiz. This was in 1876 or thereabouts—and in 1891 a number of the most prominent Southern judges and attorneys gave a written testimonial that Polock was a wonder, and they affixed their signatures to the statement—some forty or more of them.

This, as you see, was some time ago. And it may surprise you to know that this same Mr. Polock hale and hearty at 73 years of age, is teaching shorthand, down at his cottage in Frenchmen street, near Claiborne.

The house is one of those spick and span little homes, with its concrete walk, its potted plants, and its half-bowed green shutters.

You tap at the door and wait, expecting to see an aged man waiting to receive you. You picture him to yourself, as you wait—probably he will have a cane, perhaps crutches, you imagine him coming slowly to the door, with one hand to his ear, asking your business. As the time passes you think that he is probably even more infirm; and you picture him in a wheel chair, coming through the room toward the door.

But the shutters are thrown open by his wife instead, and, in answer to your question, she replies: "yes, he's here. He's out in the back yard building a chicken coop. Wait a minute and I'll call him."

And a few minutes later Mr. Polock comes briskly into the room.

Old? Infirm? Your imagination has led you astray this time. He is as spry as you are—probably more so, and he grips your hand until it hurts.

"Shorthand? Of course! But, my dear sir, no classes. I will not bother with classes. I have thirty-two pupils just now, and expect to have more shortly. I dismiss some of them, if they are stupid, for I can't bother teaching stupid pupils. That's why I won't accept money until after I've had them a while, and can see whether they can make stenographers. If they haven't any brains, I send them packing. Not worth while to try and teach them anything. And I know my business! You bet I do!"

You are almost taken off your feet by his briskness on such a hot afternoon, but before you can say anything, he is off again.

"There is only one way to teach shorthand properly, and that is to teach one man at a time. I'm willing to teach anyone absolutely free of any charge until they can read and write. I don't charge them for paper or pens either. But if they can't learn out they go! Like that!"

And there is a grand gesture of sweeping the unworthy ones out of the door.

"But—" you are beginning.

"Stay my friend!" says Mr. Polock, assuming a histrionic pose and putting one hand in his shirt front, "that is life. Those who can, succeed: the others must do something else. Ah, I know what life is. I have written a poem about it. I shall recite it to you:

Life is what you make it!
That is something everybody should know.
And those who are not acting naturally right
Had better go very slow!
Life is what we all make it!
And it will be so to the last.
And those who have acted naturally right
Will climb to the top of the mast!

He finishes with uplifted finger: "Ha! What do you think of that? I wrote it myself! That's my motto! Did you know that I raise chickens? Yessir, chickens are just like people. If people don't know how to take care of themselves, how can they expect to raise chickens, I ask you? Pip! Don't say pip to me! Diphtheria! That's what it is. Chickens have diphtheria, just as people do, and fools call it pip! The idea! Look here. Do you see this desk? It is full of bottles of chicken medicine. When my chickens get sick, I can cure them without a bit of trouble. I've had as many as 400 at a time, but I sell them. I've only got about forty now."

You interrupt forcibly this time: "But what have chickens got to do with shorthand?"

"Everything!" is the surprising answer. "Chickens are just like people and they have almost as much sense. I treat my chickens as I would treat my children if I had any. And they reward me well. They make money for me. See what I mean? It's the same with people. I try to teach them the best way I know, and the ones who succeed pay me well. It is very simple, my dear sir!"

You laugh, and your host laughs with you: "Ha! That's life!" he repeats.

"I see you are a philosopher," you hazard.

"No sir, I am not!" says Mr. Polock, "I am an inventor. Didn't I tell you that I am a member of the Parisian Inventors' Academy, and I have received a gold medal for my inventions? Here is the certificate."

And sure enough, there it is, an imposing document, with a large seal, dated 1893, and written in French.

"And what have you invented?" you ask.

"Many, many things." Says Mr. Polock, "I've been inventing all my life. Come here, and I'll show you."

He runs to the desk (the same one that contains the chicken medicine) and opens a drawer. Inside there are dozens of tubes of brightly colored paper. He takes one, pulls a rubber band at the base, and suddenly a small parachute shoots out of the other end and hits the ceiling with a bang; then it opens and sails slowly to the floor.

You stand open-mouthed in astonishment. It is a remarkably clever top: "And you invented that?" you ask.

"Just a whim," says Mr. Polock, shooting another parachute skyward. "I've never done anything with it. I invented it before the war, and I'm waiting for things to get normal again."

"But—" you are beginning when he stops you with an upraised hand.

"I know what you are going to say; you are going to advise me to hurry, or it will be too late. What is seventy-three years to me? My dear sir, I'm going to live to be a hundred!"

And, as you stand there in wonder, you believe it.

Times-Picayune, August 5, 1922, p. 4.

Editor's Note: *Solomon Lawrence Polock was married to Oney Hanora Kleppinger. He was active and teaching shorthand into his eighth decade, and died in February 1935 at the age of eighty-five.*

29

THE CHINA MENDER

Unusual Ways of Making a Living

Old, Rare China and Porcelain Made to "Live" Again Because of Almost Miraculous Repairs

It was a curious accident that led to my hearing of Miss de Lesseps and her work—an accident which occurred at a dinner.

There were six of us, grouped together at a small table, dining informally one Sunday evening—one of those cozy little gatherings which have so much charm and which one enjoys more than large and formal affairs.

We had been speaking of antique porcelain ornaments, and the subject had been suggested by two beautiful Chelsea figurines which supported bronze candlesticks, and which, in turn, supported the candles that lighted the table. Although extremely delicate, these small china figures were perfect to the last detail, and a hundred years or more had left no traces, it seemed. The figures represented a dancing couple, a boy and a girl, dressed in brilliant colors, and covered with a high glaze which reflected the candlelight.

One of the guests wished to examine the figures more minutely, and the hostess extinguished the candle and handed the bit of china across the table. But the hand that reached for it was too slow, and the ornament slipped to the table, rolled over and over, and struck a heavy silver dish. There was a tiny, tinkling crash and the head of the statue cracked off and rolled from the table's edge to the floor, while the dancer's body remained, headless, like a French aristocrat after the guillotine.

There was a moment's pause. We all realized the situation rather acutely; the statues were very valuable, very rare. They were the hostess' most highly prized possessions—she had just said so before the accident—and her collection of antique figurines was said to be almost priceless.

The girl who had dropped the ornament gave a little wail: "Oh, Mary!" she almost sobbed. "I'm so sorry."

But strangely enough, the hostess laughed: "It's not serious," she said. "It's happened before. I've done it myself and my servants have done it. It's easy for Miss de Lesseps to mend it. It will never show. The next time you come to dinner here, you'll never be able to tell where it is mended. Nearly every piece in my collection owes its condition to her."

It was after dinner that I got Miss de Lesseps' address, and I remember writing it on a card—1145 North Villere street. A week or so later I went there one evening, carrying under my arms a statue which had been broken in half.

Miss Pauline de Lesseps lives with her sisters in a small house downtown and her workroom is a revelation to the uninitiated for there she does the most intricate china mending—mending so delicate and so perfect that, when completed, there is never a trace of the break. You will find her surrounded with the tools of her trade: a dozen different kinds of cement, spirit lamps, blow pipes, glue and hundreds of implements for glazing and painting.

She has been working with fine china for years, and has mastered this most delicate art. Years ago she and her brother, George de Lesseps, began the study of ceramics and china mending, in which they established themselves a thriving business. But today Miss de Lesseps is working alone, for her brother is dead.

She doesn't like to speak of her processes, for they are secret formulas and the result of long study. The work takes infinite patience and a steady hand—and the blending of colors in repainting broken pieces, and the matching of colors in their exact shade is trying work. But Miss de Lesseps has made this her lifework and there is no bit of broken porcelain too difficult for her to mend. She is even able to mold missing parts—a hand or a foot—which has broken from a delicate bit of porcelain and which has been lost. So clever is she that one cannot detect that the article has been broken at all. But it takes time! Oh, yes.

In her workroom you will find scores of beautiful vases, dozens of ornaments—Royal Doulton, Chelsea, Derby, Majolica, Worcester, Minton—and each one requires different handling. Even Wedgwood may be mended so the break is not noticeable.

"I enjoy my work," says the china mender, as she smiles up at you from her work table, "each broken piece presents a different problem, and the work is never monotonous. I find constant joy in it. Just now I am trying to perfect a process for mending cut glass and Venetian glass by the blow pipe method, and by melting the broken edges and welding them together instead of using glue or transparent cement. I have not succeeded yet, but I shall, I think, and when I do, it will revolutionize glass mending."

Many collectors of antique china know Miss de Lesseps and though she chooses to live far from the business district her customers have beaten a path to her door. And in her cleverness lies the salvation of many a discarded ornament.

Times-Picayune, August 7, 1922, p. 9.

Editor's Note: *Pauline de Lesseps was born in New Orleans in 1867.*

30

THE HOT TAMALE MAN

UNUSUAL WAYS OF MAKING A LIVING

Maybe There Are "Doubting Thomases," But a Pushcart Affords More Than Bread for Its Pusher.

The Shades of night were falling fast,
When up the avenue passed
A pushcart, red and very nice,
Emblazoned with the strange device:
"TAMALES"[34]

HA! Fooled you that time! Thought it was going to be "Excelsior," didn't you? Well it's not. It's "Real Mexican Hot Tamales."

You've seen him, of course, the hot tamale man. He haunts St. Charles avenue every afternoon, usually near the corner of Melpomene, and he is easily distinguished by his bright red pushcart with its sign in nickel letters.

His name, if you please, is Nicholas Cancio del Valle, and he is on the avenue every afternoon, just at the time when the strongest of emotional desires – love hate and all the rest—are changing into a desire for dinner.

And, if you want to know who eats hot tamales, you have only to stand beside him for half an hour. Little shoe-shine boys, newsies, business men drop by; fashionable women in limousines call orders to their chauffeurs, and he smiles back at them as he opens his cart and spears the tamales deftly with an implement strangely like a hat pin, and then rolls them in a double thickness of paper.

Between customers, you talk with him: It's a lucrative business, he tells you, and he has saved almost enough money to open a shop on the avenue—a shop where he can make and dispense his wares. At present, he and his wife manufacture them at their home, 1300 Camp street, and they are able to sell all they can make. In winter, he sells out in no time, and goes homeward with an empty cart leaving disappointed customers behind him. For all of his customers are "reapers" he says. They buy day after day.

It wasn't always like this, though. There was a tough time at first.

"All my life," says Nick, "I have worked as a packer of fruit, in California. Four years ago, I came to new Orleans, bringing my wife with me. But I couldn't find a job. I tried farm work, but I couldn't make enough to live on. I was what you call 'up against it'—Then I thought of tamales, so I began in a small way, peddling them in the street. Another man joined me and we began to prosper, but then he disappeared—leaving nothing but debts.

"Wow! It was a hard time. They seized our furniture—what little we had, and left only an empty house. 'There's nothing to sit on,' said my wife, nearly crying. 'I'll fix that!' I said, and I did, too. I went out and got two boxes for chairs—It seems funny now, but it wasn't funny then.

"But I began working again—selling tamales—and soon we were on our feet. After that I had no more partners, and I'll never have another one. When I get a thousand dollars saved, I'll open my shop, but I'll do it alone—or rather with only my wife to help me.

"Just wait! You'll see. Next year this time, I'll be standing behind a counter, instead of pushing a cart in the street. Just you wait!"

Another car drove up to the curb, and a woman leaned out.

"How many tamales have you left?" she asked. "Can I have $6 worth. I'm giving a party—"

So Nicholas sold out his entire stock in trade and concluded his business for the day.

Times-Picayune, August 8, 1922, p. 4.

Editor's Note: *Nicholas Cancio, as he normally called himself, was born in Puerto Rico in 1874. He and his wife Della married when Nicholas was eighteen years old, and she was but sixteen. Around 1941 Nicholas finally opened his restaurant. He passed away in 1945.*

31

THE CHEWING GUM MAN

UNUSUAL WAYS OF MAKING A LIVING

Once a World Rover, Now, an Old Man, He Sells Chewing Gum on the Streets

~

Scene: Sidewalk in Common street, near the side entrance of the St. Charles Hotel. An old man sits hunched up over his small table which contains chewing gum and candy.

The old man speaks:

"Chewing gum? What's that? Oh! Sure you can sit here by me if you want to. I've been sitting here for seventeen years, day after day. James Kelman is my name.

"Yes, right here by the hotel. I've seen lots of changes in this street, lots of changes! I come here every morning at 9 o'clock and I spread out my gum and candy. At 4 o'clock I go home—What's that you say?

Crippled in Ship Accident

"Well, it's like this. Twenty years ago I was a marine engineer, and I had been one all my life. I was about 50 years old when I had the accident which crippled me. It was in Havana harbor, and the ship was sinking. I went below to open the sea cocks. But it was too late. Down she went, and I was nearly killed. For two years and four months I was laid up in the Marine Hospital here in New Orleans. And the pain was something terrible. I thought I was going to die. But I didn't you see. I got well.

"Yes sir! Spearmint? Oh Juicy Fruit? Thanks—What was I saying —Oh yes! While I was lying there in the hospital I thought about what I was going to do. I couldn't go to sea, and I wasn't going to beg. I thought about selling gum. The very day I got out of the hospital I bought a tray full of gum and candy and I came here. I've been right here every day since.

Saw Passing of Landmarks

"The hotel people are friends of mine. Yes sir! They say that I can stay here as long as I want. This used to be the Turkish bath, but now it's remodeled and it's going to be a post office. But it won't interfere with me. I'll be right here.

"California Fruit? Thank you sir!—Weather makes no difference with me. I'm here every day, just the same. When it rains, I sit back in the doorway. My customers find me, all right. You know, I like my customers. The same ones come back week after week, year after year. See that fellow who just bought from me? I've known him since he wore short trousers. Every day, every day. He looks prosperous now, like he was a member of the firm or something—He works somewhere around here, in some office, I suppose. No, I don't know his name. I don't know many names, but I talk with them all. I know their faces, and you'd be surprised how much I know about them. They say one word one day, and something else the next—It all counts up. Pretty soon I know all about them.

Everybody His Friend

"But for that matter, everybody talks to me: Newsboys, streetsweepers, everybody.

"Yessir! Thank you sir! That's an old customer that just went by—I'm 71 years old this month and there's not many things I can do to enjoy myself. But I'm a great reader. I swap the newsboys single sticks of gum for papers that they have left over, and I take 'em home.

"I've lived down in Chartres street for seventeen years, ever since I came out of the hospital, and I keep pretty quiet. I read and read. Magazines mostly. I have a room on the second floor, nice and quiet. I don't know anybody in the neighborhood—It's like this: All day I sit here and talk to the people passing by, and when I get through, I want to be quiet. So I go home and read. I look forward to the evenings, when I can sit alone with a book. In the summer I sit by the window, and in the winter by the fire. It's fine.

"Lonesome—Well, not exactly lonesome, sort of solitary, you might say, but I don't mind. You see, I'm an old man, and ever since the old lady died, I sort of keep to myself. My children are all dead too, all but one grandson, 15 years old. But he's gone off to Georgia. Not as I blame him for that—Lord! When I was young, I went all over the world in ships. Yessir!

He Is a Lover of Books

"What was I saying. Oh yes! I was talking about reading. A book is something I never get tired of. I just read one after another. Books make me forget everything. Usually I suffer all the time, but as soon as I get my nose into a book I forget everything. I don't feel any pain, and I forget I'm alive. Reading to me, is just like whisky to some men. It makes me forget everything—

"Yessir! Peppermint? Thanks!—That's another of my regular customers. I can spot them a block off. Here comes another one. Take a good look at him—

"Thank you sir!—Notice him? He just laid down his nickel and walked off with his gum. He's been doing that every day for five years. He never misses a day, and he never says a word. He's the only one who never says anything to me—Funny, ain't it?

"You know, it's just occurred to me—maybe he can't talk! For all I know he may be a dummy! I'll bet he is!

"You've got to go? Well, stop by here and talk to me again. I'm here every day—every day but Sunday, that is. Sundays I take a walk down by the river and look at the boats, or I stay at home and read. Mostly I stay at home. That's the best, after all. Good-bye!

"Gum? Yes sir. Here you are! Thanks!"

Times-Picayune, August 9, 1922, p. 9.

Editor's Note: *James Kelman died in New Orleans on January 16, 1953 at the age of 102, having outlived the much-younger Lyle Saxon by seven years. Kelman did not fare well in the Great Depression and in the late 1920s he moved into the Asylum of the Little Sisters of the Poor, on North Johnson Street at the corner of Laharpe. In 2016 this structure was preserved and renovated as an assisted living apartment complex. By the mid-1930s Kelman was again living on his own in the Bywater neighborhood of New Orleans.*

32

THE KNIFE GRINDER

Unusual Ways of Making a Living

An Itinerant With an Emery Wheel Could Have Been Wealthy, "But Why Hurry?" He Asks.

The rain patters down, a summer shower in the city's streets. Sidewalks are filled with men and women, rushing along, intent upon their own affairs. A constant stream of men passes in at the open door of a restaurant; some of them, passing, hail each other, catch arms, and dive to shelter, dodging the dripping awning. Bobbed haired girls, three under one purple silk umbrella, go giggling by, jostling those around them; the girl in the center has a dead white face, with vivid carmine lips, and the feathers on her hat are drooping with drops of moisture. Young men in white suits hurry from awning to doorway, splashing though puddles, running when they reach the crossing, their straw hats under their arms.

The street is filled with the clamor and clang of cars and motors; the police patrol goes by with its sharp staccato of gongs. Newsboys are shouting the afternoon papers, held in damp bundles against their bodies, their raucous voices are deafening as they push the papers into the faces of the passers-by.

But suddenly, through the roar of the traffic, there is heard, far-off, the soft chiming of a clock, softer through the pattering rain, and followed by twelve sonorous strokes—*Noon*!

Your shelter in a wide doorway is shared by a middle aged man in blue overalls and his bare forearms are stained with blackened grease. His face is seamed and lined, and his sandy moustache almost covers his grimly smiling mouth. Behind his glasses, his deep-set blue eyes are watching the crowd with a mirthful gleam:

"They're in a hurry," he volunteers, as you catch his eye. "But what's the use of that?"

You avoid the obvious reply and ask instead: "Don't you find it necessary to hurry sometimes?"

"I used to, but I don't hurry now," he says with a wide grin. "We only live once, and I don't know where I'm going when I leave here—No, I don't believe in hurrying through life. I want to enjoy myself. You know, I like people to take the time to be good natured. Gosh! What's the use of being a crab? What does it get you, I ask?"

This is a promising beginning, so you ask him his business. And he answers with another question:

"See all those people going into that restaurant? Well, they all cut their meat with the knives I sharpen. That's my business: I sharpen knives. There's a machine out there—Yes, the one on the Ford."

You look toward the curb, where a patient flivver stands. Behind the driver's seat is a grinding machine, with its separate gas engine, now silent and covered with a piece of canvas against the rain. The machine and the flivver constitute his whole stock in trade.

And there in the doorway, while the crowd rushes by and the rain patters around you, the knife-grinder tells his story, and in telling it he grips your attention—Somewhere in your consciousness, you think of the Ancient Mariner and the wedding guest, but even this idea fades as you listen to his tale:[35]

"My name is Skinner. C.W. Skinner, and I've been doing this for a long, long time—Ever since 1908. Maybe it doesn't seem long when you say it fast, but when the days go by, one after another—well, that's a different story. Anyway, it seems a long time to me—In 1906 I quit a railroad job. I left a $90 a month position to go into business for myself. I was tired of working for other people. I thought about it and I talked it over with my wife—Ah! That's a woman for you! She's dead now, God bless her!

"I started out with the butchers in my neighborhood, down around Burgundy and Clouet streets; and then I branched out. First, I had a little push cart, then a horse and buggy. And I always found plenty of work. I used to go all over town—way out—In 1915 I got a Ford, and the work kept on coming in. I got more and more—I used to go even to the suburbs downtown, uptown, but now I only go into the commercial district. And, at that, I get more than I can do. Restaurants, butchers—I turn away customers. I won't kill myself. It's hard work, you know; not laborious exactly, but tedious.

If my wife had lived, I would be a rich man today. I'll bet I would have $100,000. She was a real woman—she helped me with everything. But she died on me.

"I married twice after that—but I had to get rid of both of 'em. Wanted to play me for a sucker, and I won't stand for that. I guess not. You can play me for a sucker once, but not twice. No sir!" and he laughed.

"Now, I'm all by myself. My children are all grown up and married—all five of 'em. So I live alone. I've only got myself to provide for. I've got a few thousand tucked away in the bank against old age, and I make plenty for my wants, and enough to let me save a little every month.

"Gosh, what more does a man want?

"And I've got my friends, too. I'll tell you something. There's nothing in the world like a good friend. Don't I know? Why the folks I live with, down at 3137 Burgundy street are the best people on earth. They'd do anything for me, and I'd do anything for them too. You bet I would. I've lived with them for years.

"Happy? Of course, I'm happy. Any man would be happy with

friends like I've got. Friends—old friends are the best. You'll find that out when you get older. You'll see!"

He stops speaking. The knife grinder is making ready to go to his waiting machine. Someway, you are sorry. You feel that you have known him for years. And you find yourself wishing that you were one of those "old friends" that he likes so much.

He climbs aboard the flivver, and raises one knotted arm in salute. You stand in the doorway, watching him drive off through the slanting rain.

Times-Picayune, August 10, 1922, p. 17.

33

THE CROCHET TEACHER

Unusual Ways of Making a Living

The Sign on Her House is Done in Free Verse—She Teaches Crochet Work.

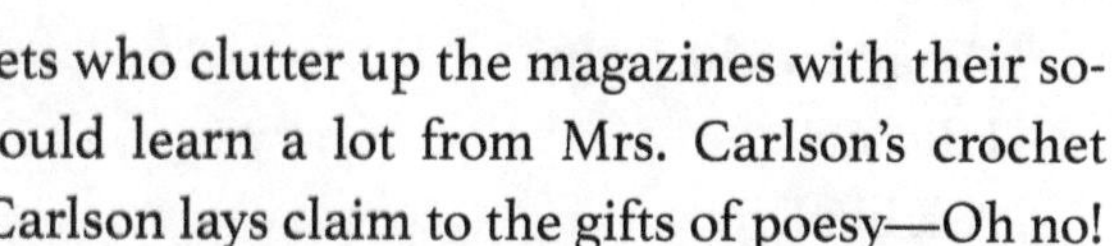

The vers libre poets who clutter up the magazines with their so-called poetry could learn a lot from Mrs. Carlson's crochet school. Not that Mrs. Carlson lays claim to the gifts of poesy—Oh no! —Her gifts are along much more practical lines. But the sign before her cottage in Clouet street is a masterpiece of free verse:

Mrs. G. Carlson's Crochet School.
Orders taken for crochet work.
Quilts made to order.
Hair work.
Mardi Gras costumes for sale here.
Cut flowers for sale.

Ladies crochet sweaters.
Hair switches.
Braids and puffs, made from combings.
Pupils taken.
Telephone!

It's the neatest little house you ever saw, with its awnings, its fresh paint, and its potted plants. You push open the gate and go in, still chanting the poetry of the sign to yourself. You knock.

The hush of a midsummer afternoon is over everything. The only sound is the cries of children, playing in an adjoining yard. As you wait, you repeat the words of the sign over and over: "Braids and puffs, made from combings—Pupils taken, telephone!"

After a pause, you knock again. And again you wait. A little boy peers at you from between the pickets of the fence:

"Do you know if Mrs. Carlson is at home?"

No answer, but a friendly smile from the child. You continue to knock. Then you speak to the child: "Run around to the back and see if you can find her."

He disappears, and soon you hear this conversation:

"Oh, Mrs. Carlson, Oh Mrs. Carlson! Big tall man to see you! Oh Mrs. Carlson!"

"What does he want?"

"I dunno!"

"Ask him!"

Then from somewhere out of sight:

"What you want, mister?"

"I want to see Mrs. Carlson."

"Well, you can't. She's in bed!"

Then a perfect babble of voices, mostly little girls:

"What you want? Mrs. Carlson's in bed. She's been operated on! You can't come in? She's getting up! Here she comes! There she is, Mister!"

Just at that moment, Mrs. Carlson appears and begins to talk rapidly:

"Well! I'm sorry to keep you waiting. Isn't it hot? I was just lying down—the hospital you know—operation. Oh, but I'm not idle. No indeed! I've been home fourteen days and I've crocheted sixteen articles! Wait and I'll show you! Thelma! Get out the things I've just made!"

And Mrs. Carlson throws open the screen door.

She is an attractive, slim woman, just verging on middle age. Her short black hair is caught back from her face by a band comb.

"Come in and sit down. Well, and to think that you want to see the things I've been making. Oh, well, they're all like that. Ask anybody in this neighborhood. Everybody admires my work. 'How do you do it, Mrs. Carlson?' they say, and I tell 'em, It's a gift of God! Yes sir! A gift of God!

Crochet Work Inspires

She raises her hand dramatically.

"I've been crocheting ever since I was 14 years old. My mother taught me, and she taught my five sisters. We're all wonderful at fancy work. But I can make it faster than anyone else. I'm inspired, you might say. I've always been that way. Thelma! Hold up those baby packets! See that. I made it in two hours! You don't believe me, I guess, but it is the truth! Yes, as I live, it's the truth.

"Oh, I'm so gifted! You have no idea. It's wonderful. I can do in one hour, what it takes the average woman all day to do. Sewing is the same. I can make a dress in no time. Quilts too! And the people I've taught to sew and crochet! At least five hundred—maybe six hundred. But I've never been able to teach one to work as fast as I can. I've been doing this, right here in this house, for twenty-five years.

They say ambitious people never get rich. I'm too ambitious. I'll kill myself one of these day, I guess. But that's the way I am, I work like lightning."

She paused for breath, while the little girl took piece after piece of lace and embroidery out of the box.

Makes Lace and Wool Roses

"See that lace: It's all handmade. I made it! One dollar and a half a yard, that's all. I can make a yard in no time—no time at all.

"And I've always enjoyed my work. My! How I like it. And my neighbors like it too. There's more than one girl that comes here every day to sew and embroider with me, making things to put in her hope chest. Yes, they've all got hope chests. Thelma! Get a quilt!"

Thelma disappears and comes back a moment later with a pretty, old-fashioned, patch-work quilt which she unrolls proudly.

"I made that years ago for myself," Mrs. Carlson continues, "and I'm making quilts all the time for somebody or other—not that I like quilts as much as crochet, but I'll turn my hand to anything that a customer wants. I like to oblige.

"Some folks have criticized me for having so many signs out in front, but I think it's only right to advertise my work. Have you ever seen wool roses like mine. No, of course not! It seems a pity to me not to put out a sign when I'm so talented—you know, I was wondering, If you ever heard of my father. He was a bar pilot, Captain Ben Ames. I was Katherine Ames before my marriage. Lots of people still call me "Miss Katherine." That is, people in the neighborhood.

"There's nobody who has finer neighbors than I have. I must say that I love my neighbors. They've been wonderful to me since I've been sick. And, after all, there's nothing like neighborliness, is there? I declare, I'm happy living here among 'em. And I know 'em as well as I know myself. I was born just a few squares from here and I've lived just in this immediate neighborhood all my life. Between my sewing and crocheting and my neighbors I never have a dull minute. I guess that's the way to be happy, isn't it?"

And then, after a little pause:

"Thelma! Bring out the false hair!"

Times-Picayune, August 11, 1922, p. 6.

Editor's Note: *Catherine Ames Carlson (her name was misspelled as "Katherine" in the article) continued her crochet and sewing business from her home on Clouet Street for the rest of her life. She died in 1943 at the age of seventy-three.*

34

THE GIRL SIGN PAINTER

UNUSUAL WAYS OF MAKING A LIVING

With Dreams Aplenty for the Future, One Woman Makes Herself Independent.

You've seen her work dozens of times—those dainty, Vanity-Fairish looking cards in show windows—those advertising cards which tell of the latest popular song, or the favorite brand of chocolates. You know the cards—dancing figures, kewpie dolls, little boys bearing trays—all that sort of thing.

For Lydia Abbott is a sign painter and a show-card writer, and she's in business for herself.

You'll find her in her office, almost any morning, at 618 Commercial Alley, in room 407—a cool, grey room with white woodwork and the only spot of brilliant color is the bobbed auburn hair of the energetic young woman who bends above the very workmanlike drawing board, wielding an air brush.

Of course, it's a mean thing to speculate upon a pretty girl's age, but, as you sit looking at Miss Abbott's slim youthfulness, you wonder at her calm, businesslike ability and her sure, straight forward work. She can't be more than 21 or so—but she's a humdinger when it comes to commercial sign work.

Unusual Ways of Making a Living

With Dreams Aplenty for the Future, One Woman Makes Herself Independent.

Illustration 9. *Unusual Ways of Making a Living No. 16. The Girl Sign Painter.* Times-Picayune, *August 12, 1922, p. 20.*

And she's matter of fact enough about it, when she talks of her work:

"My sister and I wanted to learn something that would give us a chance—something that would throw us into a real competition with men. Both of us liked to draw, and one day we answered an ad—it was in the *Times-Picayune*, by the way—of Smith the Sign Man. He advertised for girls with some talent, to learn lettering and window card work. We worked with Mr. Smith a long time. It was tedious and tiresome at first, but we expected that.

"Day after day we made the same lettering over—large and small, different types of fancy initials. We learned to do the other things that were necessary, you know the sort of training that is required; to study values and colors, and to make clean, straightforward work. After a long apprenticeship, we left Mr. Smith's workshop and each of us took a position. My sister went to the Kress store—you've seen her work in the show cards in the windows, I'm sure. I went to Beekman's. I only left him on the first of this month, because I wanted to go into business for myself, and establish a real growing concern.

"I've just started, you see, and I'm sure that I'll succeed. Although I've just gotten settled here, and haven't had time to fix up my office, the work has been coming in every day.

"Just you wait. In a few years, I'll have a big office, with lots of people working in it—"

She paused to laugh at her own ambition, and then began to discuss more intimate subjects:

"You know, my father says that it ruins any girl to go into business. They get too particular about things—their own money, and all that sort of thing. He predicts that both my sister and myself will end up as old maids."

Again that infectious laugh, and the auburn curls are brushed up out of the way. It's rather difficult to imagine Miss Abbott as "an old maid"—she's so creamy skinned, so very delectable looking.

"Perhaps," you venture, "You're not in favor of matrimony—What do think of it, anyway?"

Her teeth flash and her dark eyes sparkle: "I approve of it!" she says, quick as a flash. "In fact, I'm strong for it! And now, I'll make a confession: I've thought a lot about it!

"Did you ever read 'Man and Superman' by Bernard Shaw? Well, he points out that men never propose—that women really make the men do it. Poor man! He hasn't a chance with—I suppose, as a woman I should object strenuously to such an idea, but I agree with him. Women always propose in reality. Oh, a man may think that he takes a girl by surprise, but, believe me, he never does! It's a very stupid girl who can't arrange things to suit herself. If she's clever, she can bring the man around to the proposing point—or she can steer him so far away from it, that he never has a chance at all.

"I ought not to tell you this, it seems like betraying my sex, but it's true.

"Funny, isn't it? Girls didn't talk like this formerly, did they In the old days, when they sat at home on the sofa and waited for men to come to them, they had to be more circumspect. They couldn't tell the truth about themselves. They didn't dare: because matrimony was their only profession, their only escape.

"Well, it's all different now, and much better. See? Here I am, earning my own living—soon I'll be doing more than that—I buy my own clothes. I don't have to ask any man for money. Therefore, I can talk frankly. I don't have to be watching out for a husband to support me. It's certainly a lot better for women. It's nice to be able to say what you think.

"Oh, I've thought a lot about it. Every girl has. But not all of them will tell you the truth about it. Will they?"

Times-Picayune, August 12, 1922, p. 20.

Editor's Note: Lydia Abbott was born in New Orleans in June 1892.

35

THE COWBOY

Unusual Ways of Making a Living

Bathing Beauties Make His Mule Nervous But Bill Likes to Watch 'em —He's the Cow Puncher of Lakeview.

~

Riding out to Spanish Fort or West End almost any day you can see him—Bill Mitchell, the cowboy of Lakeview.

"Cowboy? Cowboy?" you repeat. "A cowpuncher in New Orleans? How come?"

It's like this: Bill's father is the proprietor of the Lakeview Dairy and the fine herd of Jerseys and Holsteins is the apple of Mr. Mitchell's eye, so to speak. It's Bill's job to see that the cows that browse in the high grass along the car tracks, are not run over by the Spanish Fort cars, or, as the cows also roam in the roads, that they are not run down by speeding automobiles. For the kine wander at will, taking their fill of grass and clover and of the flowers that bloom in the spring.

All day long Bill sits on the back of his mule, watching the cows at their life work of eating. Every now and then Bill and the mule make a wild dash at some adventurous bossy which has strayed upon the tracks, evidently with suicidal intent. When she is persuaded to return to the safer paths Bill slides far back on the mule, gets into the most comfortable position, and wraps himself in silent contemplation. His eyes are fixed upon the blue distance, and he is deep in thought, for all the world like St. Simon on his pillar—only more comfortable, for the mule switches its tail at the flies and, incidentally, keeps the mosquitoes off Bill's bare feet.

Bill is not very conversational—his long communions with nature have brought him into tune with the infinite, perhaps, but have not tended to make him talkative. Mostly, he answers "Yes" and "No" to your questions.

You ask him if he likes his work:

"Um hum," says Bill, crossing one bare foot over the other.

"What do you do to amuse yourself all day?"

He studies this question for a long time, and finally replies that he watches the cows.

"But don't you do something else?" you persist.

Then Bill 'lows he likes to watch the bathing beauties at Polk avenue. You ought to see 'em. Some janes. Their costumes make his mule nervous, but Bill likes to watch 'em. Lots of people do. They come out in their automobiles and watch the fair bathers who swim in the basin at Polk avenue.

Then, too, Bill likes to think. He'd have a lot more time to do this, if people didn't come along and ask so many fool questions.

Not abashed, you say: "Fr'instance?"

"Oh, lots of things," says he. "What I do, if I like to do it, and how come I'm out here."

This is so pointed that you feel you must let him understand that you get his point of view and sympathize:

"Just the sort of questions that I've been asking you?" you say tactfully.

And Bill, looking at you with interest for the first time, answers frankly:

"Um hum!"

Times-Picayune, August 14, 1922, p. 5.

36

RENTING A HURDY-GURDY

UNUSUAL WAYS OF MAKING A LIVING

The Hurdy-Gurdy is Owned by a Woman, Who Rents It to a Man—
and It Earns a Living for Both.

Want to rent a hurdy-gurdy? If so, you must call upon Mrs. Polizzi, for she owns a whole flock of 'em, and she rents 'em out. That's the way she makes her living.

Outside in the alley the rain patters down, but in the Polizzi kitchen at 319 Dryades street, all is well—for the Polizzi kitchen is also the Polizzi living room and office, and it is there that the renting of the hurdy-gurdys is arranged.

Seated by the kitchen sink, Mrs. Polizzi is drinking a bottle of pop. She continues to sip as she converses on her business, and her daughter walks up and down, soothing a crying baby.

"Yes, everybody likes the organs," say she, "mama has been in the business for a long time."

Mrs. Polizzi finishes up the last of the pop and enters the conversation, "Yes, I should say that it was a long time," says she. "Papa began it thirty-seven years ago. We've been at it ever since. See that old lady over there in the corner? That's my mother. She ran the business for a while. Now I'm running it. It's a good business, too. Everybody likes music and some days I can't keep an organ here. There's a line of men waiting for 'em."

"How much do you charge for them?" you ask.

"Oh different prices, according to the machine and the music. The new music brings higher prices—sometimes as much as $3. The older ones bring less. You can get one for almost any price you want to pay. I can let you have a pretty good organ for as low as $1.50. If you take it into a good neighborhood, you can make that much in no time. Ask Mike!"

And then, raising her voice, she calls: "Oh, Mike! Come here!"

And, out of the rain of the alley, Mike appears.

Mike is a character. Bare-footed, bearded, and wearing a battered felt hat and shirt open at the throat, he comes in smiling broadly.

"I had my picture in the Police Gazette once," he volunteers.

This is greeted by a scream of laughter by the Polizzis.

"He ain't bashful, is he?" they say in chorus.

Mike seats himself by the table and begins to peel potatoes.

"I've been grinding one of them pianos for years," says he. "You must have seen me, down there by the French Market. I've been wheeling one of them organs around for a long long time. Yes, when I began to play 'em, the popular tune was 'Daisy Belle,' just as the 'Sheik' is the popular one now. Can you remember 'Daisy Belle?' "

You assure him that your mother sang you to sleep with that tune when you were a baby, and Mike continues:

"Better men then me go out with the organs. I'm not ashamed of it. Why should I be, I ask you? Days when you get a fresh route, you make good money. Residential neighborhoods is the best. They drive you out of the business streets sometimes—they ain't got time to listen. But the people around the French Market is the ones for music. They like it."

You turn to Mrs. Polizzi: "Do you like your business?" you ask.

"Sure I do," says Mrs. Polizzi. "It's supported the whole family for a long time, and I guess it will support us for a long time to come. Ain't that so?" This last to her daughter.

The daughter, above the wails of the baby, shouts: "Yes!"

And Mike—whose full name is Salvadore Mike McGary—agrees that the Polizzis are well content with the renting of the hurdy-gurdys.

"The colored people is great for 'em," says Mike. "Lord! A ball or picnic or a fish-fry ain't complete without one of them organs!"

And Mrs. Polizzi nods assent.

Times-Picayune, August 15, 1922, p. 21.

37

THE WOMAN BOAT CAPTAIN

UNUSUAL WAYS OF MAKING A LIVING

A Woman Runs a Motor Boat Through Louisiana Bayous, from New Orleans to Grand Isle.

~

There's romance in the very name, "Grande Isle," and the history of Louisiana is full of references to this small island lying between Barataria bay and the Gulf of Mexico. Once upon a time, so the story runs, Grande Isle was the haunt of the pirates, Jean and Pierre Lafitte, and the black flag flew from the mastheads of craft which anchored there.

The island has been the scene of many tragic stories, some of them true—some of them myth, old-wives'-tales handed down in families, growing in mystery with the passing years.

Once—long ago—the island was the scene of much gaiety, for it was a favorite summer resort of the Creoles in ante-bellum times. Other islands in this group as well—and most of us have read

Lafcadio Hearn's "Chita," the story of the destruction of Isle Derniere or "Last Island" farther along the coast.

But of late we have heard less and less of the islands—although those who visited them declare that they are rarely beautiful. There was a reason for this, of course. The trip to Grande Isle was a long and tedious one—made half by water, half by land. It took an entire day, and was an arduous undertaking.

Two months ago a New Orleans woman, Mrs. E. Bertoniere of 118 North Derbigny street, conceived the idea of running a motor boat directly from the city to the island, traversing the bayous and lakes and canals, which form a "back way" to the coast, and which shortens the distance considerably.

There were difficulties, of course. In the first place the water in places is extremely shallow, boats drawing even three feet of water are likely to come to grief on the sand bar—and then, it takes a skilled pilot to make the trip through the network of small streams and tropical swamp.

Mrs. Bertoniere bought a motor boat and engaged a pilot who was familiar with that part of Louisiana. She decided to be her own captain, and to take active charge of the boat herself. And she did so. Two months ago she started and twice each week, since that time, she has set out, reaching Grande Isle in eight hours, running continuously.

Her daughter, catching the spirit of her mother, opened a small boarding house on the island, and there are now twenty guests comfortably established for the summer. And twice a week Mrs. Bertoniere makes the trip, bringing down travelers, or transporting the dwellers of the island to New Orleans.

"And I'm enjoying it more than anything that I've ever done before," said Mrs. Bertoniere. I like the open air and I like the boat. I'm sure that my business will grow and grow until I can really make something worth while out of it. I'm beginning in a small way, of course. And no matter how many men and women I accommodate I must stick to small boats, for the larger boats always run aground. I had some difficulty in finding just the sort of launch I wanted, for I got one which draws only two feet of water, and is therefore safe from sandbars.

"The trip is lovely—until I made it. I never realized just how beautiful Louisiana bayous and lakes are. It has been a revelation to many who have made the trip with me.

"And you know, you'd be surprised to know how few New Orleans people have ever visited the island. It seems strange, too, when the island is so near, and the country so beautiful."

"Mrs. Bertoniere say she feels that she is doing pioneer work in her motorboat venture, but she likes it, and wouldn't stop now for more money in other types of business.

"Liking my work means a lot to me," she says, "and this is the first time I've felt really contented with what I'm doing. Of course, I'm not making a fortune at it—you can readily see that; for the boat is small and accommodates only a few people, and I can only charge $5 a round trip—$2.50 each way. And I only make two trips a week. Yes, I go on Saturday and return Sunday; then I go again on Tuesday and return Thursday. But I'm only beginning this summer—remember that!"

Times-Picayune, August 16, 1922, p. 6.

38

THE TATTOOIST

Unusual Ways of Making a Living

Sailor Toney, the Tattooist, Will Cover Your Entire Body With Pictures of Birds, Butterflies, Snakes, Frogs, Flags, Ships or Women.

Down in Canal street, somewhere between the custom house and the river, Sailor Toney keeps a beauty shop for men.

It's a small and very modest establishment, but all day long men pass in and out—for Toney is a tattooist, and he has been in business seventeen years. In his day, he estimates, he has tattooed fully 10,000 men; some of them have had only a star or an anchor put upon their forearms, while others have been tattooed from stem to stern—from the neck to the soles of their feet.

As you enter, he is working with his electric needle upon the shoulder of a man: a man stripped to the waist and all of his exposed anatomy covered with designs mystical and awful, figures strange and brightly colored.

And, as Toney works, you study the designs upon the man's torso.

On his back there is: A star surrounded by smaller stars and butterflies, a Gibson girl, a Spanish girl with tremendous earrings and a necklace, an angel with six wings, a figure waving a flag and carrying a banner inscribed "Liberty"; there is a Chinese girl, a Japanese girl; there is a lighthouse; a girl in tights, a girl without 'em, a hula-hula girl, a girl stretching out her arms in mute appeal. A woman, raising her eyes toward heaven (and tattooed just under his arm) is inscribed "Mother!" But the most striking design is in the middle of his back; here a woman is shown clinging to a cross, and it is labeled "Rock of Ages!"

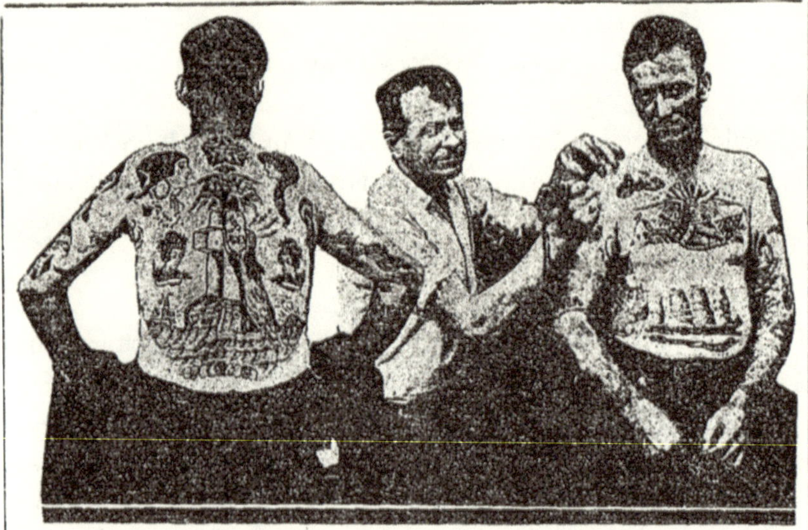

UNUSUAL WAYS OF MAKING A LIVING

Sailor Toney, the Tattooist, Will Cover Your Entire Body With Pictures of Birds, Butterflies, Snakes, Frogs, Flags, Ships or Women.

Illustration 10. *Unusual Ways of Making a Living No. 20. The Tattooist.* Times-Picayune, *August 16, 1922, p. 9.*

The man's arms are covered with red roses, a figure blowing a trumpet, a dagger piercing a rose, a figure of Columbia, anchors and stars. His chest has a large design called "America," in which there are shields, eagles with outstretched wings, and fluttering flags in red, white and blue. Below this, on his stomach, is a four-masted ship in full sail, while, lower still, there are two hissing serpents. On one shoulder there is a large butterfly, and on the other is a snake, upon which Toney is working as you look on, with wonder and admiration.

But to Toney it is all in the day's work. "Everybody likes to be tattooed," says he, as he applies the electric needle.

"Doesn't it hurt?" you ask the man whose façade is being decorated.

He nods grimly. "Sure it does!" he says. "But it soon gets well, then look what you've got!"

Look indeed! You're decorated for life!

"This fellow," Toney volunteers, "is fixing up a surprise for his wife. When she saw him last, he didn't have any tattooing, but now he's nearly covered with it. It'll surprise her, all right!"

"You bet it will," says the tattooed man.

"Funny," says Toney. "But women are always interested in a tattooed man. Some of 'em say they hate it, some of 'em like it. But they always want to see the pictures!"

You think of this startling revelation for a few minutes, wondering what would happen if one of your friends "surprised" his wife in this way while said wife was away on a vacation. The thought is too much for you, so you change the subject.

"You may think that only roughnecks are tattooed, but that's your mistake," says Toney presently. "Here take a look at my card while I finish this butterfly."

You turn the small square of green pasteboard over in your fingers, and you read: "Sailor Toney, electric tattooist, using a thoroughly antiseptic method causing but little pain or swelling. All colors and many odd designs of universal interest. Private work if desired, 205 Canal street." Then on the other side: "Why intelligent people have tattooing: Because it is an odd and beautiful form of art, very interesting and more expressive of sentiment than any other thing. It is more fascinating than costly jewelry and cannot be lost or stolen. It's a memento we can keep through life and retain after death; a sure identification in case of need or accident. Tattooing has come to stay with all classes of society! Ten kings of

Europe are tattooed, and nearly all members of royal families, both sexes!"

"Amazing!" you say.

"Ain't it?" asks Toney, putting the finishing touches on the butterfly.

"Do you ever tattoo women?" you ask.

"Sure," he answers. "There is one woman, right here in New Orleans who came to me and had a pair of black openwork stockings tattooed on her legs. It was a pretty job! Then, another time, two girls came here and had me tattoo sorority pins on their shoulders. Pretty and refined, they were, but they wouldn't give their names. Then, there's my wife, for example; she wanted a mole tattooed on her cheek, but she jumped when the needle stuck her—and now the mole is all crooked.

"But men like it. You ought to see 'em. Sailors, soldiers, marines, farmers—lots of other people. Nowadays farmers are the best customers. They come in from the country and have a design started; then they come back a month or so later and have another one put in. That's the way it goes, mostly—a little at a time. But sometimes there's a job like this one. I'm tattooing his whole body, every part, all at once. A swell job, too!"

John Feicht of Gretna, the man in the chair, stirs a little uneasily as the needle continues its work on his shoulder. "Yes," he volunteers. "I'm being tattooed all over—every part of me is being decorated. Toney's got as far as my waist now, and then he's going to do my legs and feet. I'll be a regular moving picture when he's finished. The job is costing me $350, but it's worth it, every cent. There won't be another man like me in New Orleans when he gets through."

And Toney, with an artist's pride, says that this is true. John Feicht is going to be his masterpiece.

But wait until John's wife sees him!

Times-Picayune, August 17, 1922, p. 9.

39

WOMAN COW-CATCHER CLEARS $15 DURING FIRST DAY OF APPOINTMENT

Out in the open spaces of Jefferson parish, where men are men, Mrs. Margaret Knight, cow-catcher of the Eighth Ward, began her official duties Saturday by rounding up fifteen cows.

Her first day in office was filled with feverish activity. She started out at dawn and rounded up the peaceful kine from the vales of Jefferson parish, drove them into her cow-lot back of her home—and before milking time in the afternoon the impounded cattle had been redeemed and Mrs. Knight stood upon her front steps, triumphant, with $15.

And as the slow descending sun painted the landscape with its glowing colors, she smiled and explained:

"Hot dog! I'll call it a day!"

Oh, yes, they're getting action in the Eighth Ward these days. It took a woman to bring it about. Irritated beyond measure by the meanderings of cows, irritated further because there was no water for the bossies to drink, aggravated because there was no male who would act as cow-catcher and pound-keeper for the Eighth Ward, Mrs. Knight applied to the police jury of the parish, asking why the cows were treated like that—likewise the people who lived in the path of the wandering bovines. They couldn't get a man with enough gumption to do it, said the police jury. Too much trouble ensued.

Asks for Appointment

"How about me? Will I do? I'll be cow-catcher!" said Mrs. Knight.

"Tickled to death, madam!" came the instant reply. So Mrs. Knight returned home with a new title, and with the official document which gives her the power to waylay wandering cows and fine the owners.

Interviewed at her home in Ridgeway and Fargot avenues, Metairie Ridge, Mrs. Knight told of her activities.

"I've been living out here for more than a year," said she. "My husband keeps bees, and we raise flowers and potted plants for the market—and the cows were terrible! We got no peace at all. Cows all over the place. I couldn't stand it.

"And that's not all! I'm a member of the Society of Prevention of Cruelty to Animals," she continued, "and I sent for Peter Gluck of that society to come out here and look at the water that those cows are forced to drink. Look at it!"

And she pointed to the ditch water outside, filled with green slime.

"That's all they get," she said. "When I drove those fifteen cows into my pound today they drank five big tubs of water—they were wild for it. Think how that filthy water must affect the milk.

Not Afraid of Danger

"I'm going to do my duty. If there's any trouble I'll take it as it comes. I'm not afraid!"

And she went on to explain about what cows drink. "Of course, when they're penned up in their own fields, they have good water, because we've got good water out here. When they are turned out to roam, that ditch water is all they get.

"I'm tired of seeing the people beating horses. That's why I wanted Mr. Gluck to see conditions for himself! But I've got the power now to do what's right—and to make the other fellow do the right thing! Just you wait! The next time I see an animal mistreated, I'll fix 'em."

Readers of the Times-Picayune may remember Mrs. Knight's bold exploit of catching a burglar, single-handed and unarmed, a little more than a year ago, when she and her husband were in charge of a cemetery here. That bold, bad burglar learned not to fool with a "poor, weak" woman—as he was overpowered in the tussle and was sent to jail.

As cow-catcher of Jefferson parish, Mrs. Knight feels that she has found her life-work.

Times-Picayune, March 11, 1923, p. 1.

NOTES

[1] Chance Harvey, *The Life and Selected Letters of Lyle Saxon* (Gretna, Louisiana: Pelican Publishing Company, 2003), 22.

[2] New Whatcom is today incorporated into the town of Bellingham, Washington.

[3] Harvey, *The Life and Selected Letters of Lyle Saxon*, 27.

[4] Washington State Birth Records, 1870-1935, Lyle Saxon Birth Return, April 4, 1891, retrieved at www.ancestry.com (January 3, 2018).

[5] James W. Thomas, *Lyle Saxon: A Critical Biography* (Birmingham: Summa Publications, 1991), 2.

[6] "Women Pay Tribute to Mrs. Lyle Saxon," *Times-Picayune*, March 16, 1915, 7.

[7] Harvey, *The Life and Selected Letters of Lyle Saxon*, p. 39.

[8] "At the Gates of Empire" ran in the *Times-Picayune* from April 4 to August 14, 1922.

[9] The "mauve decade" was a term used to describe the 1890s, because of the discovery of an aniline dye that was commonly used to color fashions during this period. St. Peter Street is where Saxon lived at the time the book was published.

[10] Jeanette Raffray, "Origins of the Vieux Carré Commission, 1920–

1941," *Louisiana History: The Journal of the Louisiana Historical Association*, Vol. 40, No. 3, 284.

[11] Lyle Saxon, "Vieux Carré Awakening; Is Coming Into Own Again," *Times-Picayune*, June 6, 1920, sec. 4, p. 3.

[12] Thomas, *Lyle Saxon: A Critical Biography*, 87-8.

[13] *New Orleans City Guide* (Boston: Houghton Mifflin Company, 1952), v.

[14] Compare, for example, these reviews: Edward Laroque Tinker, "Dramatic Novel of Louisiana," *New York Times Book Review*, July 11, 1937, p. 1; George W. Healey, Jr., "Novel by Saxon is Distinguished Work," *Times-Picayune*, July 11, 1937, Sec. 2, p. 7.

[15] Thomas, *Lyle Saxon: A Critical Biography*,162-3.

[16] Harvey, *The Life and Selected Letters of Lyle Saxon*, 43.

[17] "Death Sentence of Guirlando Stands," *Times-Picayune*, November 1, 1922, p. 23.

[18] Stanislsaw Frankowski, lecture in Criminal Law, December 4, 1996, St. Louis University School of Law, St. Louis, Missouri, notes by the editor.

[19] "Mother Braves Prison for Baby," *Times-Picayune*, March 24, 1923, p. 5.

[20] "Mrs. Gardiner Detained to Foil Dope Ring Plot," *Times-Picayune*, May 8, 1923, p. 4.

[21] Advertisement, *Times-Picayune*, May 30, 1923, p. 15.

[22] Lyle Saxon, "Reprieved," *Times-Picayune*, May 20, 1923, sec. 1-B, p. 1.

[23] Lyle Saxon, "Fingers in the Dark," *Times-Picayune*, May 27, 1923, Sec. 1-B, p. 1.

[24] "Prophet In Jail Again for Hitting Woman on Head," *Times-Picayune*, September 14, 1926, p. 1.

[25] The French word for ten is *dix*.

[26] Thomas, *Lyle Saxon: A Critical Biography*, 45.

[27] Ibid.

[28] Unfortunately, all who expressed the opinion that the French Opera House would be rebuilt in short order were entirely wrong. The effort was bogged down in politics and acrimony, and the French

Opera House was never rebuilt. The site is now occupied by a large hotel.

[29] This swipe at immigrants stands in odd contrast to Saxon's series published two years later entitled, "Unusual Ways of Making a Living," in which many immigrants are profiled in a positive light. It also stands in contrast to the ancestors of the Creoles who were, of course, immigrants, and whom Saxon deeply respected.

[30] Jenny Lind (1820-1887) was a Swedish soprano and Adelina Patti (1843-1919) was an Italian-French soprano, each of whom performed at the French Opera House. Sarah Bernhardt (1862-1923) was a stage and screen actress in the late nineteenth and early twentieth centuries.

[31] The word "banquette" indeed can be found in French dictionaries, but it means bench or seat.

[32] Amelita Galli-Curci (1882-1963) was a Milanese coloratura soprano who was popular in the early twentieth century.

[33] From 1898 to 1909, Collier's Magazine ran a series of fiction stories by E.W. Hornung, featuring the adventures of A.J. Raffles, a gentleman and a thief. The character was later played by David Niven in the 1939 movie, "Raffles."

[34] Saxon satirizes Henry Wadsworth Longfellow's poem, "Excelsior."

[35] In the "Rime of the Ancient Mariner" by Samuel Coleridge, a young man is having a good time at a wedding reception, but has the misfortune of being chosen by the Mariner to hear a prolonged tale. The young fellow tries to escape his tormentor, but to no avail.

ACKNOWLEDGMENTS

I wish to thank the following people and organizations for their help in the creation of this book.

First, I thank my wonderful wife, Connie Warner, for the patience and encouragement she has provided. She has been a tremendous help and supporter of this work. The Louisiana Research Collection at Tulane University was helpful in providing access to some source material about Lyle Saxon. The Williams Research Center at The Historic New Orleans Center houses a superb collection of vertical files that have been invaluable. Many images of original articles and artwork were obtained from *The Times-Picayune* Historical Archive. The New Orleans Public Library Louisiana Collection possesses microfilms of *The Times-Picayune* back issues that were also used to research these stories. Their staff, as always, was exceedingly helpful. Thanks also to Taite McLoughlin for supportive discussions on the cover design. Finally, I thank the State Library of Louisiana for permission to use the portrait photograph of Lyle Saxon, and Charlotte Bonnette at SLOL for her help.

ABOUT THE AUTHOR

Lyle Chambers Saxon (born 1891, Baton Rouge) earned his writing chops as a reporter for the New Orleans *Times-Picayune*. His style was imaginative, and commingled fact with fiction, but Saxon compensated for factual inaccuracies with an enthusiastic embodiment of the city's romantic spirit. As a young man in the early 1920s, Saxon pursued an exhausting newspaper career, writing the stories and character sketches that gave him the skills to produce later classics of Louisiana literature, such as *Children of Strangers*, *Fabulous New Orleans*, *Old Louisiana* and *Lafitte the Pirate*. Lyle Saxon died on April 9, 1946, after a long battle with cancer, and barely a month after he narrated the Krewe of Rex parade on nationwide radio for the first post-war Mardi Gras season.

(*Photo courtesy State Library of Louisiana, Louisiana Division.*)

ABOUT THE EDITOR

James Michael Warner is a native New Orleanian who travels with his wife Connie between Bay St. Louis, Mississippi, St. Louis, Missouri, and the San Francisco Bay Area. He is a member of Biographers International Organization and took his B.S., Ph.D. and J.D. from Centenary College of Louisiana, Indiana University and St. Louis University, respectively. Michael blogs about the culture, books, history, food and lifestyle of southern Louisiana and Mississippi at www.culturedoak.com.

THANK YOU

Did you enjoy this book? Please leave a review on Amazon.com.

Read more about the Cultured Oak Press and our books. Please visit our blog, *www.culturedoak.com*, where we comment on lifestyle, food, art and culture in southern Louisiana and Mississippi.

For more information, please drop a note us at:

info@culturedoak.com

The Cultured Oak Press

www.ingramcontent.com/pod-product-compliance
Lightning Source LLC
Chambersburg PA
CBHW030811310726
48980CB00006B/465/J

* 9 7 8 0 6 9 2 1 4 1 5 2 6 *